JULIA'S LAST
HOPE

JANETTE OKE

JULIA'S LAST HOPE

JULIA'S LAST HOPE
A Bethany House Publication/September 1990
The Janette Oke Collection/1997

Cover by Dan Thornberg, Bethany House staff artist.

Bethany House Publishers
A Ministry of Bethany Fellowship, Inc.
11300 Hampshire Avenue South
Minneapolis, Minnesota 55438

If you would be interested in purchasing additional copies of this book,
please write to this address for information:

The Janette Oke Collection
BDD Direct, Inc.
1540 Broadway
New York, NY 10036

ISBN: 0-553-80564-9

BDD Direct, Inc., 1540 Broadway, New York, New York 10036

Printed in the United States of America

1   3   5   7   9   10   8   6   4   2

Dedicated to the memory of
a dear friend,
Ramona J. Middleton, M.D.,
who went to be with the Lord
on February 16, 1990.
She was so much more than a doctor
to the many who knew and loved her.

JANETTE OKE was born in Champion, Alberta, during the depression years, to a Canadian prairie farmer and his wife. She is a graduate of Mountain View Bible College in Didsbury, Alberta, where she met her husband, Edward. They were married in May of 1957, and went on to pastor churches in Indiana as well as Calgary and Edmonton, Canada.

The Okes have three sons and one daughter and are enjoying the addition to the family of grandchildren. Edward and Janette have both been active in their local church, serving in various capacities as Sunday school teachers and board members. They make their home in Didsbury, Alberta.

Contents

Chapter One

The Unexpected

No one in the household was prepared for the news. Julia Harrigan was in the east parlor, her back turned to the warm rays of the Saturday morning sun. It promised to be another delightful spring day. She hummed softly as her hands worked a dainty hem in a new tablecloth and smiled as the smooth fabric, fine linen imported from England, slipped through her fingers. She did love fine things.

From the dining room came the contented sound of Hettie's low, rich singing as she cleared away the remains of the morning breakfast.

A gentle squeaking sound coming from the porch told Julia that her two daughters were seated in the double porch swing. She imagined their yellow-gold hair reflecting the morning sun, their wide, frilly skirts fanned out across the whiteness of the painted seat. Then the swing became silent, and Julia heard footsteps cross the veranda as the girls moved on to some other activity, chattering as they went.

Again Julia smiled. Life was good. God had certainly blessed them.

"Papa was wrong," she whispered, giving the needle an extra thrust for emphasis. "John Harrigan *can* support me in the manner to which I am accustomed."

Julia almost chuckled at the thought of her father's concern. She looked about her. The east parlor walls were pa-

11

pered with soft yellow roses, the furniture was white wicker, padded liberally and covered with yellow chintz. Everything about the room spoke of comfort and a family of means.

Beyond the doors, rich walnut furniture highlighted the dining room. Deep, skillfully patterned carpet covered the floor, and fine china graced the table.

The large, bright entrance hall featured a winding staircase that led to comfortable and homey bedrooms above. Pastoral pictures, gentle in expression and presenting a sense of harmony and peace, lined the hallway.

In fact, everything about the house spoke of quietness and calm. Julia had always dreamed of having a home that would convey to her family and guests strong feelings of tranquillity. Knowing this, John gave her every opportunity to create a peaceful atmosphere in their home.

Raised in the East and educated in a fine school, Julia had been brought up to be a woman of gentle spirit. But when she met the young John Harrigan, a rugged westerner, she did not hesitate to make her choice known. Even her father was amazed at the way she put her dainty foot down.

"I want to marry him," she insisted.

"Think, girl!" her father roared. "You are used to finery and ease. Do you think this rough woodsman will be able to provide it for you?"

"I really don't care," she responded. "Surely there is more to life than tea parties and silk dresses."

"Yes, there is more to life. There is poverty and need and hungry, unkempt children. But I do not wish it for an offspring of mine."

She pleaded then. "Oh, Papa. Please—I beg of you, don't send him away. I would rather have little with this man by my side than a fine mansion and someone I don't love."

In the end her father gave in, though reluctantly.

"I am thankful that your dear mama isn't alive to see you leave for that godforsaken wasteland," he whispered as he kissed her goodbye after the wedding ceremony. "She would never forgive me." His heavy sigh told Julia that he suffered because of her going.

"Come and see us someday, Papa," she pleaded. "I will write to you as soon as we are settled." And she kissed his cheek where the tears had left dampness.

So she and John moved West, settling in a remote village tucked in the Rocky Mountains. John took a job as overseer in a large lumber mill.

Julia stopped her needlework to concentrate on those early years of marriage. They had been difficult, requiring both her and John to make many adjustments. Thinking back, she was glad her father had not made a trip west to visit them at the time.

Then their lives took an unexpected turn. John's uncle came to them in need. Born and raised in the wilds, Uncle George was a salty, rough man, crude in his manners, and Julia felt uneasy around him. But he was John's kin, and when he took ill, Julia suggested he move into the spare room in the small house they rented.

By the time he died, Julia had changed her mind about Uncle George. At his simple funeral service she cried harder than any of the other mourners. She would miss him, she knew. She had learned to love him in the time that she had waited on him.

"You mustn't weep so," John cautioned as he placed his arm around her shoulders. "You must be extra careful."

Julia looked at her increasing waistline. Not wishing to harm their unborn child, she stopped her crying, straightened her shoulders, and blew her nose in her linen handkerchief.

"I will miss him," she said softly. "He really had a special sweetness about him."

"I never thought I'd hear you call Uncle George sweet," John teased. "Salty was the word you used to use for him. Remember how uncomfortable his quick, sharp tongue used to make you?" John pulled Julia into his arms. "But Uncle George surprised us, didn't he? Underneath all that, he had a sweet spirit. We both will miss him."

And then the unexpected. The old trapper, miner, lumberman, prospector, somehow, somewhere, had hit pay dirt.

Stashed away in a local bank was a large sum of money from a gold strike. No one knew about it until after his death, when John and Julia learned that he had left it all to them "as thanks for all you have done in caring for and loving a grouchy old man."

Julia cried again. John was less emotional about the windfall. He set to work immediately to build Julia the kind of home he felt she wanted and deserved.

He spared no expense. By the time the home was ready for occupancy the money was exhausted, but Julia was the mistress of a fine manor, the only one in town that had indoor plumbing and a generator to supply electricity.

By the time they moved into the house their family had increased. The child they had looked forward to turned out to be a girl with a twin sister. Julia was ecstatic. Having been an only child, she could think of no greater gift to give a child than a sibling playmate.

"They will be kindred spirits," she bubbled. "It will be great fun to watch them grow. Do you think they will be alike?"

John looked at his sleeping daughters. One baby stirred—the one they had named Felicity. In her sleep she moved a small fist and managed to get it to her mouth. She slurped and smacked awkwardly, frowning in frustration when her hand slipped from her lips.

The other baby, Jennifer, slept peacefully.

"I'm guessing they will be different," John answered, smiling down on their precious newborns. "Look at them. They are already showing their different personalities."

"I think I will like it that way better, don't you? It would seem rather eerie raising two of the same person—so to speak. Oh, John, do you think we will be good parents to them?"

"With God's help, we will figure out how to raise them," John assured his lovely wife.

The years passed quickly in the big white house. The small lumber town changed very little. A few people came and went, depending on the prosperity of the mill; but most of the people in Calder Springs had lived there for many years.

The Harrigans' morning routine seldom varied. John left the house to go to work at six-fifteen and returned after the mill whistle blew at five-thirty in the afternoon.

Julia never considered living anywhere else. She grew accustomed to the sights and sounds of the small town. The sharp, stinging wind off the icy mountain slopes in winter, the heavy mist curtain of autumn, the fine tints of green as spring slowly spread over the hillsides, the hum and bustle of the summer morning, the lingering acrid smell of the smoke stacks all year long.

John had picked a suitable site for their manor. It was close enough to town so Julia could easily walk on a nice day, yet far enough from the dust and clamor to give her the peace and tranquillity she loved.

There wasn't much entertainment in town, but Julia had never needed outside excitement or activity to make her happy. Julia and John were heavily involved in their church, and that, plus a few community and social events, was enough for both of them.

Julia held a simple but deep faith. Never had John met anyone with the strong personal commitment to God that Julia possessed. She was like a child in her trust of the Savior. John's pride in her was evident in his eyes and in the way he smiled at her.

The community developed a proprietary attitude toward the Harrigans, as though the family in the fine house belonged to the town. Their gentility added refinement to the whole settlement. "The Harrigans live just over yonder," folks would boast to any newcomer who would listen. "Hardly a stone's throw from our door. Such a fine family, the Harrigans. Such a proper lady she is—but totally without airs. Greets you on the street like any ordinary soul. Even has ladies in for tea. Fine folk."

Some may have envied Julia Harrigan her fine lace curtains and thick rich carpets, but there was no malice toward her. Julia did not flaunt her finery, and no one could have accused her of snobbery.

Julia rethreaded her needle and snipped off the fine cord with a click of her teeth. "Oh my," she whispered. "I forgot again."

John had warned her about snipping the thread with her teeth, afraid that she might damage them. Julia always intended to use her scissors, but she usually forgot until too late.

She wriggled in her seat, impatient at herself, and let her eyes move to the window. It was a lovely day. She should take the girls shopping.

Before Julia had time to lay aside the piece of linen, she heard a step in the hall. Her eyes filled with curiosity, then alarm, for she recognized the footsteps as John's—and John should be at the mill.

Julia's eyes traveled to the wall clock. Twenty minutes to eight. What could have happened to bring John home at such an hour? Letting the tablecloth fall to the chaise lounge beside her, Julia started to stand. But before she could get to her feet, John was in the room.

Julia took one look at him and fear pierced her.

"John! Are you ill?"

He stared at her blankly, making her wonder if he had heard her question. Then he shook his head slowly as he groped for the back of the chair.

Julia looked at his ashen face. She wished to go to him but her body wouldn't move.

He was still shaking his head.

"No. No, I'm fine," John said, but his voice did nothing to put Julia at ease.

"Then why are you home—at this time of the morning?" Julia probed.

"They sent us home. All of us. They called a special meeting this morning. For everyone. They made an announcement. Then they sent us all home."

Nothing he said made any sense to Julia. She fumbled to touch the linen. Perhaps the feel of it would make the world real again.

John raised a hand to smooth his dark brown hair.

He looks tired, Julia suddenly noticed, and wondered why she hadn't seen it before. *He needs a break. He's been working too hard.* Just as she was about to suggest it, John raised his head and looked directly at her. Julia saw a plea for understanding in his eyes when he finally broke the news.

"They announced this morning that the mill is closing."

Chapter Two

Twosome

"Oh, Fel! Don't talk silly," Jennifer said softly, her deep blue eyes imploring her sister.

"Only *you* think it's silly to talk about boys," Felicity answered with an impish giggle. "All the girls at school—"

"Well, the girls at school are silly, too," Jennifer interrupted. Her face flushed slightly. "You know Mama wouldn't like us—"

Felicity tossed her blond curls. "Oh, pooh! Mama's not so stuffy as all that. I'll bet she talked about boys when—"

"Stop!" Jennifer exclaimed, her face growing more red. "Mama was always a lady—"

"But ladies talk about boys, or men. It's just your notion that they are a forbidden subject," insisted Felicity, a new impatience edging her voice.

"I never said they are a forbidden subject," argued Jennifer.

"Well, you act like they are. Every time someone mentions one of them, you scold or change the topic. All the girls think—"

"All the girls think what?" Jennifer prompted Felicity, determined to know the end of her twin's unfinished sentence. Jennifer's eyes narrowed. She didn't like the direction of the conversation.

Felicity lowered her eyes and toyed with a frill on her full

19

skirt, wishing she hadn't made the comment.

"Well?" said Jennifer. "What do the girls think? That I'm stuffy? Conceited? Arrogant?"

Felicity's head came up. If the girls at school even hinted at any of those things, she would have defended her twin sister with all her strength.

"No! Nothing like that. They just think you're—well—sort of sober."

"Sober?"

"Yes, sober."

"Sober?" Jennifer repeated, as though unable to believe the accusation.

Felicity nodded again, still fidgeting with the frill.

"What's wrong with being sober?" Jennifer asked.

"Nothing. Nothing at all," Felicity quickly responded.

"Then why—?"

"It's just odd for a girl your age—our age—to be sober all the time."

Jennifer considered the charge. Perhaps she was a bit sober for her age, but most of the things the girls discussed did not interest her, and statements that sent other girls into spasms of laughter weren't even funny to her. After thinking for a few minutes, Jennifer shrugged her slim shoulders.

"Maybe I am odd," she said softly.

Felicity gave her a comforting nudge. "Oh, you are not. You just don't like boys." Then, as an afterthought, added, "Yet."

Jennifer's head came up and defiance tilted her chin. "I like boys," she declared. "I just don't see the point of making silly statements and giggling over them, that's all."

Felicity shrugged. This conversation was going nowhere, and she didn't like to be boxed in. Responding to the restlessness within her, she reached one foot to the porch floor and gave the swing another push. It had been moving much too slowly to suit her.

"Do you think Mama will let us get that green organdy for new Sunday dresses?" she asked.

Jennifer was used to Felicity's quickly changing moods

and her jumps from one topic to another. She picked up on both immediately.

"Oh, I hope so," she said with shining eyes, lowering her foot to add her push to the swing. "I have never seen such a pretty color."

"Blue looks better on us," stated Felicity, pulling at a strand of her long hair.

Jennifer nodded. It was true. But the green was so beautiful—so rich looking—and they had so many blue dresses.

"Do you think Mama would take us today?" asked Felicity, her face brightening with the thought. "It's such a beautiful morning."

Jennifer widened her eyes in support of the idea; then she placed a hand on Felicity's arm as though to restrain her from a sudden dash to the parlor.

"Mama's hemming the new tablecloth," she reminded her sister. "She wants it finished by next Sunday when the preacher's family comes for dinner."

Felicity sighed. It would not be right to ask Mama to stop her work and walk to the shops just to buy their green material.

"What should we do then?" asked Felicity, boredom touching her voice.

"I suppose we could clean our room," Jennifer suggested, giving her twin a brief sideways glance.

"We've cleaned our room," Felicity groaned.

"We've picked up our things and made our beds," Jennifer corrected. "But you know what your closet looks like—and Mama said—"

"Oh, bother!" exclaimed Felicity. "Why bring that up again?"

"Because it's still not done," Jennifer scolded.

"Just because *your* closet looks like it's never been used—"

"That's because I keep it tidy as I go," lectured Jennifer. "You could do that too if you just took a bit of time."

"Time!" Felicity exploded. "Who has time to stop and—?"

"I do. And so do you. It's much easier to hang it up or put

it away when it's still in your hand than to pick it up later."

Felicity glared. She put out a foot, stopped the swing with a jerk, and stood up. "You sure know how to spoil a nice day," she fumed.

Jennifer did not look offended. She knew all about Felicity's moods, and this one was harmless. Soon Felicity would be asking her to join in some exciting caper. Jennifer stayed seated, her hand resting lightly on the wooden arm of the swing.

"I will help you if you wish," she offered.

Felicity expected that. Jennifer was always helping someone after she had already done her own work. Felicity didn't stop to analyze the situation or even to consider herself privileged. She shrugged. "Let's get it over with then."

Jennifer stepped from the swing and followed her sister to the offending closet in their bedroom.

Jennifer took charge. She moved everything from the closet floor and placed it in a heaping pile before her sister. "Here," she said. "Sort it out. Make a pile of the things that aren't worth saving. I'll hang your clothes properly."

Felicity didn't argue. She dropped to the floor and began to rummage through her possessions. Felicity was a collector. She treasured things. How could she throw away all these items that represented a part of her life? She looked dismally at the dried wild flowers, still stuffed in a little glass vase, long since void of water. Harley George had given her the field flowers at the school spring picnic. Felicity blushed as she thought about her stammered response. And now Harley was gone. His parents had moved away. How could she throw out his flowers?

Felicity's eyes moved to the news clippings carelessly tossed in a hat box. They told about a young man from Europe who had visited their area to challenge the local mountain peaks. Jennifer and Felicity had stood on the station platform along with a number of other local youngsters and watched him and his party as they unloaded their gear. He had been so dashing! So adventuresome! For a moment Felicity had longed to be a boy—or to make him realize she was a girl. She fingered the clippings and wondered where adventure had taken Erik Eriksen after his visit to Canada.

Felicity reached for a hair bow. She wouldn't think of wearing it now. It was much too childish, but it had been a favorite. She looked at the stain on one end. Claude Singer had dipped it in the inkwell—just to get her attention. All the girls had liked Claude—but hers was the only ribbon he had dipped.

With a big sigh, Felicity scooped her treasures to her, knowing she would be unable to discard any of them. "What we need is separate rooms," she announced.

Jennifer stopped her sorting and shifting of dresses and poked her head out the closet door.

"What do you mean?" she asked. They had always shared a room even though the big house had three additional bedrooms. They had never wanted their own rooms—had never wanted to be apart. The thought frightened Jennifer now.

"There isn't enough room in this dinky closet," insisted Felicity.

"It's the same size as mine."

"Yes, but you—" Felicity stopped. How could she express the fact that Jennifer didn't have treasures without sounding harsh?

"I what?" demanded Jennifer.

Felicity fumbled for words. "You—you don't have—have as many things to put away."

"That's because I throw out the junk," Jennifer stated.

"It's not junk," Felicity insisted.

Jennifer sighed. She knew Felicity was more sentimental about things than she was. At the same time she knew that Felicity was often more impatient with people. It was people and their feelings that mattered most to Jennifer, and now it was Mama she was thinking of. Mama had asked Felicity to clean her closet, and Mama would be upset if it was not done. And Felicity might even be assigned a second chore if the first was not completed in the allotted time. Yet Jennifer hated to get caught in the middle. She had to gently maneuver, suggest, and involve Felicity, although Jennifer would have preferred to work on the mess herself. But that wouldn't set well with Mama.

Jennifer felt trapped.

"I have a little extra space on my shelf," she sighed. "Why don't we put everything you want to keep in a small box and set it in my closet?"

Felicity looked relieved.

It took some skill to fit them all in the box, but they managed to do so. Felicity still had her treasures. Jennifer stacked a few of her own hat boxes to make the extra one fit on her shelf. Finally the task was done. Felicity's closet looked as neat and tidy as her own, Jennifer thought. And there hadn't been a scene over the doing. She felt relief as she closed the closet door and suggested to Felicity that they get some lemonade to take with them to the back porch.

As they passed the east parlor they heard voices. "That sounds like Papa!" exclaimed Felicity.

Jennifer glanced at the hall clock. "He shouldn't be home at this time of day," she reminded Felicity.

Felicity tossed her head and hurried toward the door. What did it matter what time it was? It was always nice to have Papa home. Perhaps he had some delightful surprise. Perhaps—

The two girls arrived at the parlor door just in time to hear the stunned voice of their father say, "The mill is closing."

Chapter Three

Changes

"Closing? What do you mean?" Julia asked, her voice calm and even.

John's voice was not as calm as he answered her. "Closing! Shutting down! Finished!" he declared, his words tight and clipped.

Julia understood then. Not about the mill, but about John. John was worried. She had to do something to help him. She crossed the room and laid a hand on his tense arm.

"It's okay," she whispered. "It will be all right."

John sank into a nearby chair. He shook his head as though to contradict his wife's statement of assurance.

She sat beside him, her hand stroking his sleeve.

"Everything will be all right," she insisted.

"You don't understand," he argued.

"Yes, I think I do," she responded.

He looked directly into her eyes. "What did I say?" he challenged her. He had never spoken to her in such a manner before.

Julia swallowed hard. Then, with a voice as steady as she could summon, answered, "You said the mill is closing. Is going to shut down. Is finished." She found it difficult to keep her chin from quivering, her eyes from filling with tears.

"You must be in shock, just as I was. You still don't understand. But when—"

"I am not in shock," she said firmly. "I am in my right mind. The mill will close. That means you will be without a job."

She held his eyes evenly, daring him to challenge her again. "I know we will be fine," she insisted, and gave his sleeve a tiny tug, hoping to bring them both back to reality. "You can get another job. You have fine references."

"Jule—all I know is lumber," he reminded her, his voice patient again in spite of their circumstance.

"And that is enough," Julia said.

"The mill is closing, Julia." He shook his head as if to clear it. "I knew we didn't have as much lumber as we should, but this . . ." His voice trailed away; then he looked directly at Julia. "If the timber supply is gone, there will not be another mill opening up to take its place."

Julia would not be deterred. "There are still mills in other towns. There will always be mills. The world can't get along without lumber."

"The other mills already have workers."

"If there is no job in lumber—you can learn something else. You have a good mind—and a strong back. There will be other jobs—somewhere."

"Yes," he admitted, "I could—if it wasn't for the house."

"We can sell the house and buy another," offered Julia with a shrug of her slight shoulders. She hoped that John did not read the agony in her eyes. She loved their house. Their home.

He shook his head slowly, pain showing in his eyes. "I'm afraid you don't understand. Without the mill, the town will die. There will be no sale for the houses, any of them. The property will be worthless—useless. It will become a ghost town."

His words made Julia's breath catch in her throat. Her hand on his sleeve trembled slightly and her eyes misted. Then her chin lifted and determination returned to her eyes.

"God has always provided for us," she declared fervently. "He will not forsake us now—when we need Him the most.

Although the news is—is crushing, He will show us what we must do. Of that I am sure."

Her words, spoken with such conviction, eased the tension in John's face. "Oh, Jule," he whispered softly and drew her into his arms.

"You'll see. Everything will work out." She stroked his hair and pressed her cheek against his.

Neither of them saw the two girls standing in the doorway. And neither heard them retreat as they turned as one and left for their own room.

Jennifer broke the silence. Her face was ashen, her eyes filled with fear. "What will we do?" she whispered hoarsely.

Felicity had thrown herself face down on her bed and was sobbing uncontrollably.

Jennifer hastened to her and placed a protective arm around her sister's shaking shoulders.

"Shh, shh. It's all right."

"I don't want to move away," sobbed Felicity. "I like it here. My friends—"

Jennifer stroked her sister's long blond hair. "We might not have to move," she soothed.

"You heard Papa," sobbed Felicity.

"You heard Mama," responded Jennifer. "God will show us what to do. He knows all about the mill. Perhaps Papa will find another job—"

"You heard Papa," Felicity countered. "The mill is all he knows."

"You heard Mama," Jennifer repeated. "Papa could learn another trade."

"We would still have to move," Felicity argued, her sobs growing louder.

"Stop! Stop! Listen to me," Jennifer commanded, shaking Felicity by the shoulder. "Mama and Papa will hear you and they will feel even worse than they do now. We've got to think about them right now. Please stop!"

Felicity could not stop, but she did quiet down a bit. Her sobs became softer, her body more relaxed.

Jennifer walked to the window. She lifted a trembling

hand to brush aside the pale blue curtains and look out over the scene below. Her eyes scanned the street, the neighboring houses, the small town with its church spire and school yard, the mountainside that rose in the distance. She loved it here too. Tears welled up in her eyes. She would hate it so if they had to leave. Why did the mill have to close? Why couldn't things continue as they always had? They had lived here for as long as she could remember. Surely there was some way for them to continue living the life they had always known. Her hand relaxed, and the curtain fell back into place. Jennifer squared her shoulders and turned to Felicity. "If we have to go—we must make it as easy for Mama and Papa as possible."

Felicity brushed at her tears and nodded her head.

"You can take your treasures with you," continued Jennifer, trying to console her brokenhearted sister.

A fresh torrent of tears ran down Felicity's cheeks. "But I—I can't take my friends or—"

"But if everyone has to move—perhaps our friends will be going with us," Jennifer said to her sister.

"Where?" Felicity sobbed.

"I—I don't know. To wherever we have to go. To another mill. Their papas work in the mill too," Jennifer reminded Felicity.

Felicity began mopping up. She wiped her eyes and blew her nose noisily. Jennifer was glad that the worst of the storm was spent. She crossed to her sister and laid a loving hand on her shoulder.

"We'll be all right," she assured Felicity again, wishing with all her heart that she felt as confident as her words sounded.

Felicity nodded. She pushed herself up from the bed and straightened her skirts. Then she went to the dresser, picked up a hairbrush, and brushed her hair into place. "I'm going to go wash my face," she told Jennifer. When she returned a short while later she showed no trace of her tears.

Jennifer wished that she could dismiss the incident as easily. Inside, she still felt knotted, twisted. In spite of her brave words to Felicity, she did not feel assurance about their future.

"Let's ask Mama if we can go get that green—" began Felicity.

Jennifer stopped her with a quick shake of her head. "Not now!" she exclaimed. "Papa has no job."

Felicity looked surprised, as though she had already forgotten their circumstance, but then her eyes softened and she nodded her head in agreement.

"I guess that would be unthinkable," she finished lamely. "Well then, let's ask if we can go to the drugstore for a soda," she continued. "Surely we can still afford that."

Jennifer gave her a dark look, and Felicity stared back at her.

"Felicity Harrigan," said Jennifer sternly, "we are thirteen years of age. Surely we can be understanding when our parents are in trouble."

Felicity shrugged. "Okay, okay," she said impatiently, "so what are you going to do to make things right, Miss Know-It-All?"

"I—I don't know it all," stammered Jennifer. "I—I just know that we can't be asking for things when Papa is without a job. There will be no money—"

Felicity's eyes brightened. "That's it!" she squealed, and threw her arms around Jennifer's shoulders.

"That's what?" questioned Jennifer.

"Jobs! We are old enough to have jobs. We can help Papa."

Jennifer held herself in check for a moment; then she hugged Felicity in return.

"Of course!" she agreed. "Of course. We can find jobs."

"Let's not tell them," suggested Felicity; "not until we each have found a place to work."

"But—" began Jennifer.

"We will talk to Hettie. Tell her that we are going up town for a soda and she can tell Mama."

"But—" began Jennifer again. She would not lie—even to conceal their plans of helping the family.

"And we *will* get a soda," continued Felicity, walking to

her dresser and opening a drawer. "Here," she said, producing some coins. "I have enough for a soda. It's from what Papa gave me last week."

Jennifer had never known Felicity to keep any of her spending money. But there were the coins in her hand. It reminded Jennifer that she too had money stashed in her drawer. But even as she thought of it she decided to leave the money where it was. Who knew how soon her papa would find another job? Perhaps her money would be needed for things other than sodas.

"Okay," she finally conceded. "Let's go see Hettie."

As they proceeded to the kitchen, Jennifer's mind was troubled. Never before had they made their own plans and gone off to the drugstore without asking permission from their mother. Jennifer hoped that Felicity's idea—as good as it seemed—did not get them both in trouble.

Chapter Four

Sharing

The news of the mill's closing had traveled fast. The whole town was in shock. As Felicity and Jennifer sipped a common soda at the drugstore they heard the somber, low voices of men and the frightened, shrill voices of women. It seemed to be the topic of all conversations.

"What on earth will we do?" they heard one woman ask. "We were just getting back on our feet after all of those medical bills. Now this."

Her friend tried to be reassuring, but her own voice broke as she answered, "I guess we'll have to go elsewhere. Start over."

"Start over?" questioned the first, her voice quivering. "We're too old to start over."

"What you plannin'?" a man asked his neighbor.

"Don't know. Just don't know," answered the second. "Right now my wife is sick. I came to pick up some medicine. Doc says the change might be good for her. The smoke here has always bothered her."

The first man nodded. "Maybe it will," he agreed, but there was doubt in his eyes. What good was a change if there was no money with which to buy the needed medicine?

"Came at a bad time," said a third man.

"For everyone," agreed the first, his eyes heavy with the worry of it.

As they listened to the people talk, Jennifer and Felicity sensed more than ever the seriousness of the situation. Their problem was not an isolated one. The whole town was affected, just as their father had said. What would happen to all of them? Was there anything two young girls could do?

It was Jennifer who shook them from their despair.

"If we are going to find jobs, we'd better hurry," she whispered to Felicity. "Everyone our age might soon be looking for work."

Felicity stopped flirting with the young man stocking the drugstore shelves and jumped to her feet. Jennifer was right.

"You take this side of the street and I'll take the other side," she ordered Jennifer and then quickly reversed her decision. "No, you take the other side, I'll take this side." It would be wonderful if the druggist needed more help to fill his shelves, she was thinking.

But the druggist was not interested in another clerk— not even a soda jerk. He smiled at Felicity and shook his head sadly.

"Don't know how much longer I'll be here," he admitted. "Not the right time to be hiring."

All of the merchants along the little street said much the same thing. No one was hiring. Felicity pushed back her hair from her warm face and trudged on. She hoped that Jennifer was having better luck. When the girls met at the end of the main street, however, Jennifer's report was no more encouraging than Felicity's.

"We'd better get home before Mama starts to worry," said Jennifer.

Felicity reluctantly agreed. Besides, she was thirsty, and they had spent all of her money on the soda.

"We mustn't say anything about the mill closing when we get home," Jennifer warned. "Mama and Papa will want to tell us at the proper time."

Felicity nodded and waved to a friend across the street.

Everything was quiet when the girls reached home. They found Hettie in the kitchen serving late-morning coffee to Tom, her husband, who worked the gardens and was general caretaker around the manor. Both looked unusually serious but brightened when the girls walked in.

"You lookin' for a snack?" asked Hettie. Although she had never had children of her own, Hettie had a knack for understanding them. She always knew what the girls wanted and needed.

"Do you have more lemonade?" asked Jennifer, hoping that her voice sounded unconcerned and normal.

"I sure do," answered the older woman, patting Felicity's golden head as she passed her.

"And you, missie?" she asked Felicity.

"The same," responded Felicity without much enthusiasm. Tom lifted his head as though curious, but made no comment.

"Cookies?" asked Hettie. "Got some fresh gingerbread."

"Just lemonade," said Felicity.

"So what has taken the starch outta you?" asked Tom, his hands cradling his coffee.

"We just shared a soda," Felicity answered. "Where's Mama?" She almost asked for Papa as well, but caught herself in time.

"In the garden," Tom answered.

The two girls thanked Hettie for the lemonade and left for the garden. It seemed important to see their mother. They had to know how she was.

Julia was attacking the rose bed with all of the energy in her slim body, singing hymns in her rich soprano as she worked. Jennifer and Felicity exchanged relieved glances and smiled at their mother as she turned toward them.

"Where have you two been?" asked Julia, halting her song long enough to pose the question.

"Didn't Hettie tell you?" asked Felicity.

"Since when is Hettie your messenger?" Julia responded, stepping back to study the two faces before her.

"We just went to the drugstore," offered Felicity.

"I have no objection to your going to the drugstore—when you have permission to do so," Julia replied evenly.

Both heads dropped.

"Sorry, Mama," murmured Jennifer. She had known they would get themselves in trouble.

"You know the rules of the household," went on Julia. "Permission is always needed to leave your own yard. I don't think that is too much to expect. Do you?"

Two heads shook as one.

"In the future, you will see that permission is granted—first," stated Julia.

This time the two heads nodded.

Julia turned again to her rose beds, and the girls went back to the house and sat in the swing. Jennifer squirmed on the wooden seat, but Felicity had already forgotten the scolding.

"I cleaned my closet," she called to her mother.

Jennifer sucked in her breath.

Julia lifted her head. "I'm glad to hear that," she responded.

"It's as clean as Jennifer's," went on Felicity.

"Good," said Julia.

"Do I get a reward?" asked Felicity.

"Indeed!" said Julia, and Felicity's eyes sparkled.

"You may join us for dinner tonight," Julia finished.

"But I always—" began Felicity, then felt the nudge of Jennifer's toe.

"Exactly!" responded Julia, and turned back to her roses, singing as she worked.

After dinner, John lifted the family Bible from the bureau and turned the pages absentmindedly. He knew he had to tell the girls about the mill, but he wasn't quite sure how to do it, what to say. True, changes were in store for all of them—but what changes?

He knew Julia was right. Of course God would care for them—just as He had always done. But God had assigned the care of the family to the father of the home, and John felt as if he were failing his family. Even though he was not responsible for the closing of the mill, he still felt the guilt. He wanted to supply for the needs of his family as he had done in the past.

Though he tried to appear confident, his shoulders sagged. He had spent the afternoon with other men from the lumber mill, and the conversation always came back to the same stark truth. There would be no work in this small town once the mill closed. And there would be no sale for property—no matter how fine it might be. The little town of Calder Springs would soon be a ghost town.

Julia reached for John's hand and tried to encourage him with one of her confident smiles—though deep within her heart she felt little confidence.

John found the place where they were to continue their scripture reading and cleared his throat. He read the story of how Jesus fed 5,000 people with one young boy's lunch, and Julia found herself wondering just how many times in the future Christ would need to multiply the loaves in her cupboard.

The girls listened attentively to the scripture verses. Even Felicity seemed to be concentrating on what her father read.

John closed the Bible and laid it aside. He cleared his throat, and Julia knew he was searching for words.

"Before we pray," he said at last, "we—I—there has been some news that has come to us—your mama and me—today that we need to tell you about because it affects all of us."

Jennifer looked down at the bows on her shoes. One was crooked. She bent to twist it to its proper position. Felicity stirred restlessly beside her. Jennifer straightened and gave her sister a silencing look.

"We—we may be having some changes in our lives," John continued, and Julia nodded pleasantly, as though changes were always nice.

"The lumber mill has run out of trees to process in this area and is going to move on to—to somewhere else."

Jennifer could not bring herself to look into her father's eyes. Felicity stirred again, and Jennifer placed a cautioning hand on her arm.

Julia remained silent, allowing John to say what he had to say in his own words—his own time.

"That means there will no longer be work for me here," he finally managed.

If he expected an explosion of some sort, he was mistaken. The room was silent.

He waited a moment and then went on. "We might have to give up our home here and move to another town," he added.

The girls sat rigid.

"Do you understand what I am saying?" John asked the girls.

They both nodded.

"We will be fine," Julia put in, giving the girls one of her special smiles.

"What will we do till Papa finds work?" Felicity asked, directing her question to her mother. Julia's eyes clouded.

"It won't take Papa long to find work."

"But everyone uptown says they can't hire now. They don't know how long—"

Jennifer gave Felicity a jab.

Felicity stopped short, her eyes filling with horror.

John and Julia studied the two faces before them.

"You knew?" asked John.

Felicity nodded.

"They went to the drugstore today," explained Julia. "I should have realized—the whole town must be buzzing."

"How much did you hear uptown?" John asked.

"Actually," Jennifer replied slowly, "we—we knew before we went uptown. That's—that's why—"

"We went uptown to try to find jobs," blurted Felicity. "But everyone said they would be moving soon and couldn't hire anybody. Everyone."

Julia's eyes filled with tears. "You went uptown looking for work?" she asked.

"We just wanted to help until Papa found work again," Jennifer apologized.

John looked shaken. "That was good of you," he managed to say. "But I hardly think my little . . ." He hesitated when he saw their disapproving looks. "My two young ladies," he corrected. "I hardly think that my two young ladies need to look for work—quite yet." He managed a weak smile.

"So how did you hear the news?" Julia asked.

Felicity spoke again. "We heard Papa's voice and wanted to see him, so we went to the parlor, but he was telling the news about the mill, so we left again."

"I see," sighed Julia.

"Let's pray together," John said, reaching for his wife's hand, as he always did for family prayer.

They bowed together. John had a difficult time voicing his concerns for the future and skirted the issue with a general prayer. He needed time to talk to the Lord alone about his worries. Maybe after he had worked through the situation he would be able to discuss the future more openly with his family.

Julia's hand tightened on his. She understood his tension.

———

Two weeks. Two weeks of work remained for every mill worker in town. After that the mill would be no more. The machinery would be dismantled and moved to a new location.

Two weeks. Two weeks to make plans—to bolster oneself for the many changes that were sure to follow.

Some men handed in their notices, drew their wages, and left, hoping to find jobs elsewhere before the rush. Others stayed and put in the few hours that would earn them one last paycheck. Then what?

Chapter Five

The Plan

"Hettie, is the parlor set up for tea?" Julia asked her housekeeper.

"Yes, ma'am," the woman nodded.

"Where is Rose?"

"She's in the kitchen making extra sandwiches."

"Good. Did she get all my invitations handed out?"

"All but the one for Mrs. Pruett. She's gone to see her mother."

"Good," said Julia again. "Did Rose say how many we can count on coming?"

"Said most folks seem right anxious to be here," responded Hettie. "We expect most all of them."

Julia nodded. Her stomach was churning. She had never set out on such a venture before. She wasn't quite sure how to go about it now—but something had to be done.

"Did Rose tell everyone two o'clock?" Julia asked anxiously.

"I believe your invitation told them that, ma'am," Hettie reminded her.

"Oh, yes. Yes, of course," Julia responded, her cheeks slightly flushed.

Hettie busied herself with the tea service.

"Oh, Hettie, I am so nervous about this," Julia admitted,

lifting trembling fingers to her cheeks. "What if it all goes wrong?"

"Well, now, what could go wrong? You are simply having neighbor ladies in for tea—and while they are here you will discuss your—our—problem and see if anyone has any ideas how it might be remedied. Nothing difficult about that. Neighborhood ladies always talk about neighborhood problems."

Hettie made it sound so simple. "We'll need to get right to it," Julia said, casting a nervous glance at the clock. "It won't be long until the ladies will need to go home. We only have an hour or so until school will be dismissed."

"You can talk about a lot of ideas in an hour," Hettie said to comfort Julia.

Julia hoped so. She also hoped the women would be on time. Just as she was about to begin pacing, the doorbell rang. Hettie ushered in Mrs. Wright, the preacher's wife.

"Oh, I am so glad you were able to come," said Julia, taking the woman's hand. "I may need your help. I don't know how to do this—this sort of thing."

Mrs. Wright held Julia's hand firmly. "Don't be nervous," she whispered, "just pretend you are leading the missionary women's group at church. You always do such a nice job."

"Thank you," Julia returned, managing a smile.

The doorbell continued to ring until fourteen ladies were gathered in the spacious Harrigan parlor. Hettie and Rose busied themselves serving tea and dainty sandwiches, followed by flaky pastries. Julia studied the clock and then the neighbors before her. The news about the mill hung heavily about each of them. An unfamiliar seriousness shadowed their faces, a darkness veiled their eyes, and their shoulders sagged under the invisible load. In spite of their attempts to be casual, Julia knew they felt every bit as anxious as she did.

She rose to her feet and cleared her throat.

"You all know that I have invited you here for more than just tea today," she said candidly. "Though it is a treat to have the fellowship of good neighbors, we all share a common

burden at this time. I—I don't know if there is anything—
that we—as women—wives—can do about the situation our
husbands are in—but I thought maybe—if we put our heads
together—we might come up with something."

All eyes focused on Julia. All ears listened carefully.

Julia shifted her weight from one foot to another.

"Now then—we know this is a lumber town. That we have
no other industry to keep us going. But is there—is there
any other possibility? I mean—what might this town be able
to do for—for commerce?"

They searched one another's faces. Each woman seemed
to be looking to a neighbor for an answer, but no one was
finding it.

"We must think," said Julia with such urgency that her
brow puckered and her hands twisted before her.

"Without the mill I don't see much hope," ventured a
somber-faced woman.

Several in the circle shrugged in agreement.

"Let's look at what we *do* have," Julia suggested. "Hettie,
would you bring that chalkboard, please?" With the easel
beside her, Julia continued. "What do we have here?" she
asked the women.

Blank looks clouded faces.

"We can't farm," said one woman frankly. "These mountains hardly leave room for a small garden."

"But we do have gardens—all of us," replied Julia, and
she wrote "Gardens" to get things started.

"We have some wild berry patches scattered here and
there," one woman ventured, and Julia added that to her list.

"We have more'n our share of mountains," offered a timid
young woman.

"Mountains," said Julia, writing the word in big letters.
"Lots of people love mountains. Now—what do people go to
mountains for—besides lumber?"

"Restin'," answered an elderly woman almost hidden in
a corner.

Julia stopped with her chalk suspended. An idea was beginning to form. She wasn't sure if it was crazy—or feasible.

But she had to share it with her neighbors.

"Do you—do you suppose we could make our little town into a—a resort town?" she asked breathlessly.

"Don't have much for a hotel," commented the banker's wife.

Julia shook her head. It was true. The only hotel in town was in sorry shape. It was used mostly as a boarding place for unmarried, often transient mill workers. The owner had never bothered to "fancy up" the place.

"Well, maybe we could—could use our own homes," Julia ventured.

Eyes moved about the room. They traveled over Julia's thick carpets, rich velvet draperies, expensive paintings, china cups, and silver service. No one spoke but each of the women knew what the others were thinking. Julia Harrigan had the only house in town that visitors might pay to stay in.

"Well, we might not be able to handle many at a time," Julia went on, "but the train will continue to pass through. If we could just advertise—then we could—could set up attractions and tours and cottage industries."

"Such as?" probed one woman.

Julia lifted her chalk again. "How many of you can knit?" she asked. Eleven hands went up. "Crochet?" asked Julia. Nine responded. "Sew?" All hands were raised, though some hesitantly.

"See—it's not impossible. And we can cook—and bake—and grow our gardens and make jam from those wild berries. We could make this a real tourist town if we tried."

By now Julia's face was shining with the possibility. Others seemed to catch the spirit.

"Do you really think—?"

"Would there be enough—?"

"How could we advertise—?"

Questions began to flow. Julia had no ready answers, but she did have interest. Would it really work? Could it?

"We need to think about this some more," she said. "I know the children will be returning from school soon and you need to be home—but let's think about this and meet here again next Tuesday.

"And spread the word to your neighbors," Julia suggested. "If—if it seems workable, we will form committees. There will be much work to do. It will take all of us—working together."

It was a different group of ladies who left Julia's house than had gathered a short time earlier. Dull eyes now had a sparkle. Worried brows were smooth again. Dark shadows had disappeared from faces. Where only despair had been, there was now hope. Frail, fragile hope—but hope nonetheless.

"Hettie, do you think Mama's plan could work?" Jennifer asked a few days later.

"Why not?" responded the older woman. "Your mama is a capable woman. When she puts her mind to something, it is likely to happen."

"But people around town are saying it's a crazy idea—just a silly dream," Felicity dared to state.

"An' who's sayin' that?" asked Hettie, her eyes flashing.

Felicity shrugged. "I don't know. I just heard—"

"Well, you don't listen none to such talk. You hear? Folks should at least give your mama a chance to prove herself."

"I sure hope it works," said Jennifer slowly. "I like it here."

Hettie sighed as she lifted a pan of corn bread from the oven. She liked it too, and if the town folded, as folks said it was sure to do, she and her Tom would be without work along with everyone else.

"Well, your mama has been doing all she can. She has sent off a number of letters to see what kind of interest there might be in a tourist town here. We have about as nice a location as one could want. Beautiful mountains, pretty lakes, nice fishing streams. Your mama has summed it all up in her letters."

"But tomorrow is Papa's last day of work," Felicity reminded Hettie.

"Not quite. A couple dozen men will be working for a while yet, tearing down the mill. Your papa still has work until that is done and the machines are shipped out of here. He says that it will take him another two or three weeks to get all that done."

"But by then everyone else will have moved away," pined Felicity.

"Not everyone," replied Hettie.

"Well, most. Some of our friends have left already."

"Some folks don't have much faith," said Hettie.

Jennifer lowered her head. She wasn't sure just how strong her own faith was, but she wouldn't admit as much to Hettie.

"Here's your milk and corn bread," Hettie offered. "Stay here in the kitchen with it so you won't bother your mama. She's busy with her letter writing."

"What's she writing about now?" asked Felicity.

"She's still trying to find someone who would be interested in buying the hotel and giving it a face-lift."

"That old thing?" said Felicity. "Who'd want that?"

"Well, if this becomes a tourist town that 'old thing' could be worth a lot of money."

Felicity shrugged and lifted her milk glass. She wasn't convinced.

Julia and her committee worked doggedly. A number of the ladies had reconsidered Julia's idea and decided that her plan, exciting as it sounded, was just not feasible. They had families that needed to be fed and clothed *now*—they could not wait for some future venture to pay off. Julia's committee now consisted of just eight ladies—eight determined ladies bent on saving their town, their homes, and their dreams.

Chapter Six

Baring the Heart

Julia straightened her bent shoulders and pushed back a wisp of wayward hair. She had always loved gardening. Had always filled her flower beds with summer flowers. Had always planted a garden to supply her family with fresh vegetables. But the plot she worked over now was much bigger than any she had taken on before. She was thankful that Tom had prepared the soil for planting. Already her back ached and her knees felt bruised from kneeling.

She stood up and removed the glove from her right hand. *I'm almost half done with the planting*, she told herself, hoping to feel a sense of accomplishment. But all she felt was weariness. "I have over half of it to do yet," she sighed, unable to keep from stating the negative way of looking at it.

She lifted a hand to remove her garden hat and tossed the hat to the wooden bench under the lilac bush.

"I need a break," she admitted. "I think I'll see if Hettie has a cup of tea."

Julia went directly to the kitchen, stopping only long enough to get rid of her gardening shoes. Hettie hated to have dirt tracked into her spotless kitchen.

"My, you look exhausted," Hettie said in alarm when Julia stepped through the kitchen door.

Julia smiled. "Guess I'm not good for much when I can't even plant a garden," she admitted with a chuckle.

45

"You've always had a garden—just not a whole farm, that's all," Hettie replied in defense of her employer.

"Well, I decided it was time for a cup of tea," Julia admitted and crossed to the kitchen sink to wash her hands.

"It's a shame Tom can't help more," went on Hettie.

"Poor man! I shouldn't have had him doing all that spading. How is his back?"

"An embarrassment," admitted Hettie. "He feels so bad that his back gave out and you have to do the plantin' yourself."

"Now you tell him not to worry about that," Julia said firmly. "Besides I plan to get myself some help. As soon as the girls are home from school I'm going to teach them to plant. Their young backs can bend much more easily than mine."

Hettie nodded as she bustled about the kitchen preparing the tea.

"Oh, Hettie," Julia moaned, her voice low and worried. "I won't mind the work one bit—if it—if it just works out."

Hettie placed the pot of hot tea on the kitchen table and took the chair opposite her mistress.

"You're still worryin'?" she asked.

"Well, I try not to—but—frankly—I have no idea if anyone will ever want to come to our little town for a vacation. If it doesn't work—I've got these poor women believing in a dream that can never be. It would be better if—"

"Now you stop your fussin'. At least you're tryin'. No one will fault you if it doesn't work out."

"I've prayed and prayed," continued Julia, "and I'm still not sure I'm doing the right thing."

"Well, if it isn't, you can still do as the others. Quit and move." Hettie made the comment with a bit of contempt for those who had so easily given up.

"Oh, Hettie—if you only knew the times I would have gladly quit and moved. Even now I—I would be glad to go if—if only it wouldn't be so hard on John."

Hettie's eyes looked up to study Julia's face above the teapot she held.

"Do you know the first thing that came to his mind when he told me the news?" Julia asked. "The house. Leaving the house. I hadn't known how important it was to him until then. If—if it wasn't for that—I'd move tomorrow. There are other houses."

The creases in Hettie's forehead deepened.

"Oh, I know," Julia hurried on. "I love this house too—but for me it—it isn't the house that brings happiness. It's the ones you share it with."

Hettie nodded and passed Julia her tea.

"You see, I've always lived in a big house. Bigger and more elegant than this one. We—we rattled around in it. After Mama died there was just Papa and me and the servants—and Papa was rarely home. Do you know what, Hettie? I used to love walking along streets where the houses were small and crowded together and children played in tiny yards and mothers leaned over fences to chat with one another. I listened to the laughter and the chatter—and even the childish squabbles—and I envied those people until I was ashamed of myself."

Julia stopped to stir sugar into her tea, tears forming in the corners of her eyes.

"It wasn't that I didn't enjoy all the nice things in our big house," she went on. "It's just that it—it wasn't as important as having a family to love. But Papa—Papa always felt that fine things were so important—and he taught me to appreciate nice things too. But if I have to do without one or the other—things or family—things don't seem very significant."

Hettie passed her mistress a linen handkerchief and Julia wiped her eyes and nose.

"John never had a big house—or nice things. His folks pioneered on the prairie. He spent his first years in a sod shanty. He was twelve years old before they even had a wood floor, he told me. His mother had to carry water from the stream and carry chips for her fire. She did her laundry in a big tub—on a metal scrub board. Even after they moved into the wood house—with real glass panes in the windows—she still had none of the things that make life easier."

"Many women did that," recalled Hettie, thinking of her own mother.

Julia sipped the sweet tea from her china cup.

"For our first few years—I did it too," admitted Julia, thinking back. "It really wasn't so bad. A lot of work—but I had the time to do it. Although John never let me carry the wood or the water. He always got up early to carry in the day's supply before he left for work. It's funny, but I have never felt as loved and cared for as I did in those first few years."

Embarrassed by her own comment, Julia stirred on her chair. "I—I don't mean that I don't feel loved now," she explained quickly. "John still looks after me in every way—but we shared and planned in a different way then. We only had each other. John—John looked after me, and I—I cooked and—and did his laundry and cleaned his house. We didn't have you for the kitchen—or your Tom for the gardens—or Rose to help with the cleaning and serving. I guess there is a different feeling when you do the caring for each other—with your own hands."

Hettie nodded that she understood as she poured Julia more tea.

"You know, Hettie, if my girls don't have all the nice things—if they have to rough it just a bit with—with the man each chooses to marry, I won't feel sorry for them. If they really love each other—if they work together to make a home—even a small, simple place that is their own little haven—if they care enough to seek the happiness of each other—then I will consider them blessed.

"I have been blessed—more than I realized," Julia continued. "I have had both. A lovely home and a loving family. Maybe I have had more than my share. Maybe I haven't had the sense to be as thankful as I should have been. God forgive me if I have taken it all for granted."

Hettie was about to defend her young mistress again, but Julia kept talking.

"Well, no more. I have sorted out many things in the last

few weeks. This I know. God is still in charge of my life. He knows what I need and what is just pleasant baggage. If I must forfeit the baggage—I will not pout. But since it is important to John, I will do my best to hold things together—for him—and for the girls."

Julia stood up and brushed her hands over her coarse gardening skirt.

"Now, I must get back to the planting," she said, "if we are to have that big garden we will be needing."

"But shouldn't you—?"

"I will only plant a couple more rows before lunch," Julia answered Hettie's unfinished question. "Then I will wait for the girls to get home. It will be good for them to know how to plant a garden. I had to learn on my own. They should know how to do such things—and they might even learn to love it."

Julia smiled at Hettie and moved toward the door.

"Thanks for the tea." Then she hesitated, one hand outstretched to the doorknob. "And thanks for the listening ear," she said softly. "I needed to talk. I guess I still miss my mother."

After the door closed softly behind Julia, Hettie allowed her own tears to fall.

————

Jennifer and Felicity were thrilled to learn that they could participate in the planting.

"I will make the rows and you can drop in the seeds and cover them," instructed Julia, and both girls squealed with delight.

"Now change into one of your play dresses and meet me in the backyard."

The girls soon rejoined their mother, eager to get started. Julia was already stretching the cord from one stake to the other to mark a new row. She liked things neat and orderly and would have been ashamed to have a garden with vegetables growing in crooked lines.

"Can we take off our shoes, Mama?" called Felicity.

"Your shoes?" exclaimed Julia.

"Please," begged Felicity. "The Carlsons all had their shoes off when they worked their garden. We saw them. The dirt doesn't get in the shoes then."

"But your stockings will get filthy," Julia argued.

"You take off your stockings too," Jennifer explained to her mother.

Julia frowned. "Isn't it awfully hard on your feet?"

"Janie says it feels great," answered Felicity.

"Very well," agreed Julia. "If you must—then remove your shoes."

Both girls hurriedly took off their shoes and stockings. But Felicity and Jennifer had never run about barefoot before, and their tender feet did not find the lumpy garden dirt as pleasant as did Janie Carlson, who spent most of her summer enjoying the outdoors without shoes or stockings.

Jennifer winced as she made her way across the soil, and Felicity gave her a deep frown. "They'll get used to it," she whispered hoarsely.

Jennifer nodded. This was a new adventure, and if she spoiled it, Jennifer knew that Felicity would be cross.

"Now," explained Julia, "come here, both of you, and I will show you how to scatter the seed. One of you will plant, and the other will cover. Then you can change jobs."

After a mild argument, the girls decided that Felicity would plant first. Both girls bowed over the open row while Julia showed them how to plant evenly, sparingly, so that the seed would grow properly. Then Julia demonstrated the careful attention needed in covering the seeds.

"This is important work," she told the girls. "It must be done carefully and well if we are to have a good garden."

The planting began. Felicity traveled along the row on her hands and knees, dropping the seeds with careful precision. Jennifer followed, raking the soil gently back over the seeds, then patting it down to bed them.

It wasn't long until Julia saw that Jennifer was limping, but she said nothing. The work carried on. Then Jennifer was at the edge of the garden, sitting on the grass as she replaced her stockings and shoes. Julia still made no comment, but she heard Felicity whisper, "Softy!"

"You wait," answered Jennifer. "You're on your knees, crawling along on your skirt. Wait until you have to walk on this stuff."

The three worked on. Julia expected the girls to plead for release, or at least to find an excuse to take a break from their work, but to her surprise they seemed to enjoy the task. Though Felicity too donned her stockings and shoes after a few trips across the garden soil.

"How long did Janie say it takes to get used to it?" Julia heard Felicity ask Jennifer.

"She didn't say," whispered Jennifer.

When Julia had designed her final row, she leaned on her hoe and watched Jennifer scatter carrot seeds and Felicity cover them with dark, warm soil.

"You've done a good job," she informed the two. "It has gone so much faster with all of us working together."

Jennifer straightened and rubbed her back. "Are we done?" she asked.

"For now," answered Julia. "We will plant the rest when the weather is a bit more certain. We don't want frost to catch our new plants."

Felicity finished covering the last few seeds. "When will they start to grow?" she asked impatiently. "A couple of days?"

"Oh my, no!" laughed Julia. "But perhaps by next week some of them will be showing."

Felicity's face fell at the thought of such a long wait.

They put away the garden tools and went in to prepare for Hettie's evening meal. John would soon be home, and Julia wanted his womenfolk to greet him as usual in clean and orderly fashion.

.

Chapter Seven

Adjustments

Jennifer and Felicity made frequent trips to the garden. Julia was amazed at their interest. Wild whoops greeted the first glimpse of fuzzy green. Their hard labor was bearing fruit.

"The girls are growing up," mused Julia. "They still sound like children when they express their glee, but they are able to find enjoyment in doing a task—even a hard one."

Julia decided that the girls should be given additional responsibilities to help run the household.

"You know that I have sent off letters advertising our home as a place for summer guests," Julia said to the girls at breakfast one morning.

They both nodded in reply, remembering the many times their mother had instructed them not to talk with their mouths full.

"Well, we will all have more work to do when guests arrive," Julia continued.

"Who's coming?" asked Felicity, for the moment forgetting that her mouth was not empty.

"Well, no one—yet. I mean—I do not know of anyone yet. But it is still early. The advertising has hardly had time to be seen. But when—when we do have guests, we all will have to help. There will be extra cleaning, and laundry, and jobs in the kitchen."

Julia saw concern, then interest, then excitement in the twins' eyes. "What do we have to do?" asked Felicity candidly.

"Well, I thought I might make a list of chores, and each of you can pick the ones you'd like to do."

"A whole bunch?" asked Felicity, a frown appearing. Jennifer's elbow nudged her.

"Not a whole bunch. Some. And it will depend on how many people are here," explained Julia.

"I'll collect the rent," offered Felicity, her eyes shining, and Julia and Jennifer both shared the joke.

"It won't be rent, really," explained Julia. "They will only stay for a short time—so it will be—fees, I guess. Lodging fees."

"I'll wait for the list," said Jennifer.

"Will there just be big people?" asked Felicity, her eyes holding Julia's.

"Perhaps not. I have said that we have three bedrooms and so could take families," Julia answered.

Felicity and Jennifer exchanged nervous glances. "Will we need to share our things?" asked Felicity.

"Your own private possessions, no. But the porch swing and the playhouse, perhaps. Tom is going to build a sandbox and a teeter-totter. We want the children to have something to do. The parents will enjoy their stay more if their children are happy," Julia explained. "Then perhaps they will want to come again—and tell others who might also enjoy visiting a quiet mountain town."

————

John supervised the dismantling of the equipment at the mill and watched as it was loaded on boxcars and moved down the tracks to be set up at another location. It wasn't until he stood watching the train roll from view around the bend of the mountain that the reality of it all settled in. Work at the mill had come to an end.

There was nothing to do but draw his final wage and go home. He had decisions to make. Difficult decisions. He had been holding them at bay—begging for time—but he could delay them no longer. He had to face reality and find a way to provide for his family. He was proud of Julia. He hadn't known that she was made of such "strong stuff." She had rallied the town women, determined to fight to save her beautiful house on the mountainside. The house meant a lot to Julia, John reasoned. She was used to fine things. But John had the sickening feeling that no matter how hard she tried, she would end up brokenhearted. There was no way enough people would be drawn to Calder Springs. They had Banff, already becoming a major tourist attraction. And farther up the Rocky Mountain chain was Jasper. It too was growing in popularity. People already knew about Banff and Jasper, and there were only so many people with money to spend at resorts. There would be no additional dollars to spend in their little town, John figured.

It might have been different if they could have built up a clientele slowly, but no one in the town had money to cover their needs while they waited. The town would die. The rest of the people would be forced to move out—just as some had already done.

John sighed deeply, his shoulders sagged. It was hard for him to see Julia lose what she loved so much. It was hard to face the fact that the girls—who had been born to plenty—might now have to do without.

He himself knew all about hardship. He could live simply. But his family? Except for the first few years of their marriage, John and Julia had lived well. And the girls had never known hardship.

It sometimes bothered John that it was Uncle George's money that had built the grand house, not money he had earned through his own hard work. But he had never begrudged Julia the house. She deserved it. He thanked God for the miracle that made it possible. He always thought of Uncle George's money as a miracle.

John recalled his secret dream of one day owning a business of his own. He had never told anyone. Not even Julia, for he deemed the dream impossible—selfish. Uncle George's money had been a temptation—but only for a brief moment.

He would not have considered using it to fulfill his own ambition. Julia's house was always uppermost in his mind.

Still, on occasion, he thought about that little business. A woodshop. A place where he could take the rough wood that came from the forest and shape and polish it until it shone like glistening dark gold beneath his fingers. He loved the touch of wood—the smell—the pattern of its grain.

If they could have sold the big house—even for a fraction of what it was worth—they might have had a possibility of starting over. As it was, they would lose the house, lose everything. John's jaw twitched and his eyes hardened. It would be tough giving it all up. He tried to shrug off his dismal mood.

"As Jule says," he reminded himself, "God didn't pack up and move off with the mill. He's still here—still looking after us."

John headed for the office to pick up his check. Time was passing quickly and he'd be late for the evening meal if he didn't hurry.

———

Julia stopped by the bedroom where the girls were preparing for supper.

"How about wearing your blue gingham dresses tonight?" she asked them.

Two sets of eyes lit up. "Are we going out?" asked Felicity.

"No."

"Are we having guests?" asked Jennifer.

"No—it will just be us." Then Julia answered the question that she could read in their faces. "They're Papa's favorite dresses," she explained.

Jennifer turned to study her mother. Julia also was wearing one of John's favorite dresses.

"Will Papa be feeling sad tonight?" she asked.

Julia tried to keep her voice steady, her chin from quivering. "He—he may be. Just a bit. The mill is gone now. Papa hated to see it go. This was a hard day for him."

Jennifer's face grew serious. Felicity looked more buoyant. "Should I tell him my joke?" she asked.

"I'm not sure he will be ready for jokes," Julia said softly. "Just try to be cheerful—and as agreeable as you can be. No fusses."

Both girls nodded.

Julia closed the door quietly behind her as she left the room.

"I think I should tell him my joke," insisted Felicity.

"What joke?" asked Jennifer.

"A man had twins and they were both the same size and had the same color hair and the same color eyes, so how did he tell them apart?"

Jennifer looked dubious. She slipped her blue calico over her head and then asked the question Felicity was waiting to hear, "How?"

Felicity whisked on her own blue dress, her eyes sparkling in anticipation of the punch line.

"The boy wore britches and the girl didn't!" she exclaimed, then laughed uproariously at the humor of her story.

Jennifer did not even smile. "It's silly," she declared. "Silly and stupid."

But Felicity was still laughing—so hard that she could not tie the bow of her sash.

"It's silly," Jennifer said again.

Felicity's face sobered. "You're just cross 'cause you didn't think of it," she challenged.

"Am not," Jennifer shot back. "I'd never tell such a silly joke."

"You never tell any jokes at all," Felicity threw at her. "You are so—so sour—and—and dull. You never even laugh."

"I laugh when things are funny."

"No, you don't. You never think anything is funny."

"I do too," Jennifer declared. "When Papa tells a funny joke—I laugh."

"Papa doesn't tell jokes."

"He does too."

Felicity shook her head. "He hasn't told a joke since—since—"

"Well, he used to tell them. And he will again when—"

Jennifer stopped as her tears began to fall. Would Papa ever tell jokes again? Would he ever laugh and play with them? Would he ever tease Mama good-naturedly? When would their world get back to normal again?

"See! You don't even know how to laugh. You just cry," Felicity taunted.

Jennifer slapped her.

———

Julia was not at the door to greet John when he arrived home. She was in the bedroom settling the dispute between her daughters. Both girls were in tears, and Julia herself felt ready to cry. She had wanted a warm, serene welcome for John on this most difficult day. Hettie had fixed his favorite dinner, and Julia had groomed herself to please him. The girls were to have presented themselves in their father's favorite dresses, hair carefully combed, happy faces inviting him into the warmth of the family circle. But it had all gone wrong.

"Poor John. Poor, poor John," wept Julia.

Chapter Eight

Hard Work

The scene that greeted John as he entered his home that night did more to lift his spirits than Julia could have imagined. Weeping daughters and a distraught wife reminded him in a very real way that he was still needed.

His eyes lifted to Julia's tearfilled ones as he wordlessly asked the reason for the fuss. Julia shrugged weary shoulders and her tears increased. He nodded her from the room, followed her out and shut the door softly behind them.

"What's the problem?" he asked, turning Julia to face him.

Julia blinked back her tears. "It's just—just a little spat over some silly joke." As soon as she said it she realized that it was really much more than that. "Oh, John," she sobbed, leaning against his broad chest. "I thought we could have a special night to—to—" She couldn't say "celebrate." The day's events hardly called for a celebration. "To show our thanks that we are here—together," she finished lamely. "I wanted your favorite dinner, a happy family, the girls in their prettiest dresses—but the girls—the girls—" Julia burst fully into tears and buried her face in his shoulder, the sobs shaking her.

John held her and stroked her back to ease her tension. He still didn't understand what the trouble was all about.

When the tears began to subside John spoke again.

"Should I discipline the girls?" he asked.

Julia jerked to attention, her eyes opening wide. "Oh my, no," she quickly responded. "That would spoil our dinner."

John pulled her close again.

"It's so strange," Julia murmured against him. "I thought they had become—so—so—grown up. They worked so hard—and so well in the garden with me. Why, I've been thinking that they are now young ladies. I was all set to enjoy their company—their help—and then—all of a sudden—this." Julia sniffed.

"Have you forgotten their age?" John asked, patting her shoulder. "They're only thirteen. I don't think anyone knows at that age whether she is an adult or a child. Remember?"

Julia shook her head. She couldn't remember. She had been forced to go from childhood to adulthood when her mother died.

"I do hope you are not implying that I'm going to have to live with this—this fluctuation—for some time," Julia said as she wiped her eyes and blew her nose on a lace handkerchief. A sparkle of humor had returned to her eyes.

John nodded.

"Oh my!" exclaimed Julia. "We'll never know from one minute to the next whether we have children or adults!"

"Would you like me to talk to them about this incident?" John's arm tightened.

"No, I will," Julia said softly, straightening her shoulders. "You wash for dinner. Hettie will be anxious to serve us before the meal gets cold."

John kissed Julia on the forehead. Then he released her so she could speak to the girls.

Julia found two contrite young ladies sitting solemnly on their beds. Their tears had ceased, though the traces remained.

"Wash your faces and prepare yourselves for dinner," Julia said in a calm voice. "And after you have apologized to each other, you may join your father and me in the dining room—where I will expect you to conduct yourselves as young ladies. Understood?"

Both girls nodded.

Julia left the room and went to inform Hettie that she could serve dinner.

The meal turned out to be a joyous occasion in spite of the preceding event. Felicity did not tell her joke, but John told a few. The family needed something to laugh about. Even Jennifer smiled.

After the evening meal and the family devotional time, the girls led their father to the large backyard where they proudly pointed out the growth in the family garden.

"See, Papa, this is one of the rows I planted!" Felicity said excitedly. "It's peas."

"I planted the row beside it," Jennifer added, her voice more controlled.

"My peas look a little bigger," Felicity boasted. "Don't you think so, Papa?"

John was not to be drawn into such a foolish argument. He eyed the rows of peas. "They all look healthy to me," he observed. "I can hardly wait to taste them."

They returned to the house. The girls were sent to bed, and Julia picked up her handwork. John settled himself at the small desk in the library and drew out his account book. He had one more paycheck—and a number of bills to pay. Would the money go far enough? Would there be any left over to care for their needs in the days ahead?

John figured and refigured, but the numbers always came out the same. After the bills were paid, there wouldn't be much left. He pushed the book aside and left the room, snapping off the light with an impatient gesture.

Julia was still in the parlor, her handwork spread across her knees, her fingers fluttering silently as she turned a skein of white thread into an exquisite doily.

John's thoughts were miles away, but he tried to act interested in Julia's project. "What are you making?" he asked.

Julia lifted the doily for him to see. "It's for our tourist craft shop," she answered, an edge of excitement creeping into her voice. "All the ladies are making things. We're working hard to get it stocked as quickly as possible."

So, John thought, *Julia has not given up her dream.*

"We are getting quite a selection of items," Julia continued. "You should see the lovely lace collars Mrs. Shannon has made. And Mrs. Clancy has specialized in calico aprons—beautiful things. Mrs. Adams is working a quilt. She has already made two crib quilts. One in pinks, the other in blues, and—"

"It's been a long day," John interrupted. "I think I'll head up to bed." It hurt him to hear how hard the women had been working on a dream that would never be any more than that. John wondered whether he should be honest with them or let them continue to work and hope. The work did keep their spirits up.

Julia laid aside her crocheting and lowered her hands to finger the fine silk of her gown. Her eyes sought his.

"Is your last paycheck enough to cover the accounts?" she asked.

John nodded, and Julia sighed in relief.

"The garden will be ready shortly," she hurried on. "And I have another piece of material on hand for new dresses for the girls. Hettie is good at making stews and soups so the—"

"We're all right," John tried to assure her.

"Mr. Brock says there is plenty of wild game in the woods," Julia felt compelled to add.

John had often hunted in the local woods and knew that animals were plentiful.

He reached a hand to her, and she stood. "We're fine," he said again.

Julia was unconvinced. Looking directly into John's eyes, she pleaded, "If there is some way—any way—that we can cut back—make do—you will tell me, won't you?"

John saw the seriousness in her face and he loved her for it. He leaned to kiss her forehead. "I'll tell you," he promised, and then closed his eyes against the pain of the dreadful thought. He would do almost anything rather than tell his Jule that she had to find ways to cut back.

———

Spring passed into summer. The eight women on Julia's committee continued their industrious labors. Each week they placed more items on the shelves in their little craft store. Julia laid aside her plans to use the new linen tablecloth herself. Instead, she pinned a price tag in one corner of it and placed it on the merchandise shelf.

Soon they would be receiving requests for accommodation in their new resort town. Those who had extra bedrooms had them ready and waiting—with outdoor-fresh linens on cozy beds, newest towels hanging on door racks, and shining windowpanes behind freshly laundered curtains.

But with every mail delivery, letters requesting accommodation were conspicuously absent. In spite of brave smiles and determined brightness, morale began to sag. They tried not to let it show—but it was there, dogging their footsteps, causing them to add more water to the soup pot, less meat to the stew.

For Julia it meant more feverish involvement. Her efforts increased. More letters written. More doilies crocheted. More hours spent coaxing and caring for her garden.

John walked the streets, pretending that he would soon find work—but deep in his heart he knew that the town had no jobs to offer.

Jennifer and Felicity were like yo-yos. One day the enormity of the family's situation would have them down. The next day, something as small as a smile from a boy could have them up again. For Julia every moment was as fragile as spun glass. She never knew when something might snap—when she might snap. The strain was almost unbearable.

Two more families moved away. The residential streets looked deserted. Houses were boarded and left. No children played skip-rope in those front yards, no weekly laundry fluttered on wire clotheslines, no smoke curled lazily from the chimneys.

Julia hated to pass the empty houses. Where there had been neighbors, now there was only emptiness, nakedness, pain. She avoided looking at them and hurried past as quickly as her clicking heels would carry her.

Downtown was even worse. The butcher had packed his cleavers in wooden crates and thrown his stained, worn apron in the garbage can. "Can't stay any longer," he muttered. "Got a wife and family to feed."

The library closed, as did the bakery, the tailor, the blacksmith. Even the doctor shook his head sadly, packed up his wife and two small sons and left for places unknown.

"Go see Charlie," he told his grim-faced patients. "He can at least give you some shelf medicine."

But Charlie Rennings, the druggist, shook his head. He didn't know enough to become the medical advisor for the town. Nor did he know how long his little drugstore would endure.

The grocer stayed. His shelves were not filled with the same variety of merchandise as in the past, but he still stocked the basics—flour, sugar, salt, coffee. He hoped the women were right—that the tourist trade would come to their small town. Yet, he wondered if people could hang on until then.

There was still the railroad and the post office. Surely they won't abandon us too, the people reasoned. But had they admitted it to one another, their dreams were often haunted by the prospect of days without trains.

And then one day late in July it happened. Julia hurried past the closed-up buildings to do her meager shopping. On the way home she stopped at the post office, and there it was, a white envelope bearing a return address of Toronto. Julia hastened from the building and took refuge on a bench by the railroad track.

Her fingers trembled as she tore open the envelope and withdrew the single sheet of paper. She had difficulty reading, for tears blurred her sight.

At length she calmed herself enough to scan the brief letter. It was a request for accommodation—"for myself, my wife, and three children," the letter stated. Julia's tears spotted the ink before she arrived home to show John.

Chapter Nine

Hope

The Harrigan household was not the only one in town to welcome the good news. The remaining families were all excited about the prospect of their area becoming a tourist town. Activity increased everywhere. Women worked extra long hours to add handcrafted merchandise to the little shop. Men wielded paint brushes and hammers, cleaned up board fences, and repaired broken walks. Boys were sent to mow the lawns of vacated neighborhood houses. Girls swept the walks.

"No one wants to come to a ghost town," Julia told her committee at their weekly meeting. "We must do all we can to make it look as if the town is still alive."

Heads nodded, but every woman in the group knew it would be hard to disguise the fact that most folks had already deserted Calder Springs.

The women agreed that Julia would take the first house guests.

"We want them to get a good impression so they will tell others," Mrs. Greenwald announced to all who would listen.

No one disagreed.

"The rest of us need to be ready at all times for business." The group had been encouraged by a second letter that came soon after the first. The Greenwalds too had the promise of summer guests.

"Too bad we can't do something about Main Street and all those boarded-up buildings," sighed young Matilda Pendleton. The empty town was adding to her discouragement. She was about to suggest to her husband that they board up their own house and move elsewhere, but she did not make her confession to the ladies of the committee.

"We should have asked permission to use some of the buildings for our crafts," said Mrs. Clancy. "It would have kept them in better repair—and we could have arranged a small space at the front that would have kept Main Street more—more active and entertaining to our guests."

"Couldn't we still do it?" Maude Shannon asked. "There's nothing but a few boards covering those store fronts. My Jim would be glad to pull nails. Says he can't stand to even walk down the street."

Julia was tempted to voice her approval, but propriety overcame the notion.

"It's a wonderful idea—to use the buildings, I mean." Then quickly added before the ladies bolted to send their husbands forth with hammers in hand, "But we'll need the owners' permission. Mrs. Clancy—your husband is town clerk. Could he give me the names and addresses of the owners of those buildings so I might write letters asking permission?"

"I'll ask him," Mrs. Clancy offered.

"I'll get them in the mail right away," Julia promised. The ladies finalized plans for the arrival of the first customers, drank tea, and departed to fulfill their various duties.

The big day finally arrived. Julia sent Tom to the train station to fetch the guests. Mr. Clancy had a fine buggy that had been washed and polished for the occasion. They had talked of using Mac Pendleton's team of blacks to pull the buggy. They were the prettiest horses Julia had ever seen. But they were also the most spirited. Tom shook his head emphatically when Julia suggested them.

"Not iffen I'm drivin'," he stated flatly.

Julia was about to suggest that Mac do the driving when she remembered that the black team had bolted even with

Mac at the reins, giving him the ride of his life and scaring the townsfolk half to death.

"We'll use our own bays," Julia said instead, and Tom nodded with relief.

Everyone in town waited anxiously for the whistle of the afternoon train. Julia was a bundle of nerves. John knew better than to hang around. He took the hedge trimmers and went out to prune neighborhood hedges—to keep the town looking "lived in."

Felicity and Jennifer hovered around, their eyes big with the excitement of the hour.

"Did you raise the windows in the guest rooms?" Julia asked. "We do want them to smell that fresh mountain air."

"Yes, Mama."

"Did you fluff the towels?"

"Yes, Mama."

"Did you smooth the beds?"

"Yes, Mama."

"Did you dust the furniture one last time?"

"Yes, Mama."

"Did you check the flowers to be sure they are fresh?"

Felicity sighed. "We did all that—you did all that—over and over."

Jennifer's jaw dropped when she heard Felicity's sassiness, but she had to admit to the truth of the words.

Julia did not scold Felicity. She too knew the words were true. Without comment she moved toward the kitchen.

The girls headed for the porch swing. "Now she will go and pester Hettie with her questions," Felicity whispered to Jennifer. "Did you polish the silver? Did you prepare the tea trays? Did you—?"

"Don't be mean," ordered Jennifer. "She's just tense. This is very important, you know. If it doesn't work . . ." Jennifer left the sentence unfinished.

Felicity shrugged. She knew it was important. But she also wondered at times if all this fuss would really help.

"Maybe it wouldn't be so bad to move," Felicity said carelessly.

Jennifer frowned.

"Josie says she likes the new place where they live," Felicity defended.

Jennifer was well aware of what Josie had said in the letter she had sent after her family moved. It had made even Jennifer a bit envious.

"Well, Mama and Papa don't wish to move," Jennifer stated.

"But why?" Felicity dared to ask.

"I guess they like it here," Jennifer said with a shrug.

"I like it here too," Felicity began, and then sighed. "At least I used to."

"And they like the house—and the mountains—and the neighbors." Jennifer tried hard to think of as many reasons as she could to dispel Felicity's doubts—and her own.

Felicity looked around her. The house was nice, the mountains were pretty. But neighbors? Felicity's eyes widened. "We hardly have any neighbors anymore," she argued. "All of our friends have already moved."

"We still have Millicent," Jennifer reminded her.

"Pooh!" cried Felicity, jumping to her feet. "Millicent is—is dull. She—she talks with her mouth full and she—she scratches in public and she—"

"Shh," admonished Jennifer. "If Mama hears you she'll send you upstairs."

"I don't care," Felicity stormed. "I miss all my friends. I miss the shops and the ice-cream parlor and the—"

Jennifer placed a restraining hand on Felicity's arm and tried to hush her once more.

Felicity shook it off, tears forming in her eyes.

"It's not fair," she cried. "It's just not fair."

Jennifer took charge. "Do you think Mama and Papa like it?" she challenged. "Do you think they wanted the mill to close? The people to move away? Do you think they like having to make do? To open our home to—to strangers? Do you think they are never scared—or lonely? They lost friends too."

Felicity's noisy sniffling abated. She shrugged her shoulders and wiped her nose, then settled back on the swing and continued to mope. Jennifer said no more. She reached out her foot and started the swing in motion. They sat together in silence for some time before Felicity spoke again. This time her voice was low, her tone confidential.

"Jen, I'm going to hate living in a ghost town."

"That's why Mama is working so hard," Jennifer reminded her. "So that it won't be a ghost town. So that it will—will come alive again. With tourists and—and interesting people and—"

"Jen," said Felicity, halting Jennifer's flow of words, "do you think it will work?"

Jennifer stopped short, thought for a minute, then answered honestly, "All we can do is try."

"But what if—what if we don't like the people who are our guests?" asked Felicity.

"We—we need to make them feel . . ."

"At home?" prompted Felicity.

"No. No, better than that. Like they're special, Mama told the ladies. We need to make them feel like—kings and queens, Mama said. Then they will go home and tell their friends—and the town will be okay."

Silence again.

"What if—what if they are—grouchy—and—and stupid?" asked Felicity.

"What if they are nice—and exciting?" Jennifer countered.

"Do you think they might be?"

Jennifer shrugged. "Why not?"

Then she continued with a statement she knew would intrigue her sister. "Maybe they will even have handsome sons."

Felicity could not keep the laughter from her blue eyes, and it spilled over to her pouting mouth and curved it into an enchanting smile. Then the giggle came. Jennifer had hoped that it would. In spite of Jennifer's usual propriety she joined her sister in a moment of mirth.

"Do you s'pose our first guests will have a son?" giggled Felicity.

"We'll just have to wait and see," teased Jennifer, and they leaned against each other and laughed some more.

———————

John was torn. He wanted Julia to keep their lovely house. He wanted her hard-fought battle to be victorious— the venture to succeed, the town to be revived, but he had to admit that things looked grim.

Funds were very low. If it weren't for Julia's big garden— if Tom and Hettie hadn't agreed to work for room and board—if Rose hadn't moved away with her family, if they didn't get free firewood from the old mill site—if—

But John tried to be positive. The first guests were soon to arrive. Julia was sure that many more would follow. She was even concerned about where they would house them all once they started coming. She had already sent letters to former shop owners, asking for the use of their buildings in exchange for proper upkeep. With the shop doors opened, their simple space filled with baked goods, canned wild jams and jellies, handcrafted doilies, quilts and aprons, perhaps— just perhaps, folks would enjoy a stroll down Main Street once again.

In the meantime, he would keep it looking as neat as he could. Snip, snip, went his clippers. From vacated yard to vacated yard, he snipped his way. The Martins, Browns, Carltons, and Schnells. All neighbors just a short time ago. Now gone. He didn't even know where many of them had relocated. He hoped they had found work. He knew the pain of being unable to provide properly for a family.

Snip. Snip. What if the venture didn't work? How long could he let Jule pursue her dream before he stepped in? Would it crush her? Snip. He could never build her another house like the one they had now. Should he suggest sending her and the girls back east to her father while he tried to get established again? The thought made John cringe.

"If only I knew what to do," he sighed for the hundredth time. "If only I could be sure."

And then, through the sharp, clear afternoon air, reverberating from mountain peak to mountain peak, came the distinct, distant cry of the coming train.

Chapter Ten

Guests

Julia met her guests at the front door. Hettie stood a few steps behind her, her starched white apron glistening in the afternoon brightness, her nervous smile well in place.

"Good afternoon, Mr. Hammond, Mrs. Hammond," Julia said, her tone and smile indicating more confidence than she felt. She held the door open for them and allowed them to enter the spacious entrance hall.

Mrs. Hammond smiled, almost, and nodded. Mr. Hammond did not even acknowledge Julia. He was busy studying the curved stairway, the oriental rugs, the art on the walls.

Mrs. Hammond soon joined him, her eyes traveling carelessly over her surroundings. Julia shifted uneasily from foot to foot and cast a nervous glance Hettie's way. Julia's home had never before been so openly and critically appraised.

Mrs. Hammond moved forward just enough to peer into the main parlor and give it a quick assessment. Her children followed her. Julia was certain they acted out of nosiness, not interest. Their rudeness annoyed Julia. After all, this was still her home. But instead of being rude in return, Julia turned her attention to Hettie.

"Hettie, will you show the Hammonds to their rooms, please?" Then, trying another smile, Julia turned to the Hammonds. "I'm sure it has been a long train ride. You will wish to freshen up before tea. It will be served in the main parlor in fifteen minutes. Thomas will bring up your luggage."

Tom was not used to being called Thomas. His stern face showed that he did not like it now. But he said nothing, only nodded and picked up two of the many suitcases and turned to follow Hettie and the guests.

Julia paused long enough to breathe a quick prayer. This was going to be much more difficult than she had imagined. The Hammonds dressed and bore themselves as though they were accustomed to elegance, to opulence. "Used to being pampered and served too, I imagine," Julia said under her breath. "They will take my lovely home for granted and expect it to be at their disposal."

She shook her head and lifted her chin. "In which case— we shall pamper them and serve them, and they shall—shall be made to feel at home. No, not at home. I will never let them feel that my home is theirs. They are only guests here."

With renewed determination Julia went to the kitchen to prepare tea while Hettie finished helping the Hammonds get settled.

The guests were not in the parlor in fifteen minutes. Julia flitted about impatiently. The tea was getting cold. She sent Hettie to the kitchen to boil water for a fresh pot. "But don't make it until they actually show," Julia suggested.

After thirty-five minutes Mr. Hammond appeared. He had changed his traveling suit to something unlike anything Julia had ever seen. It looked very casual—very rugged— and very expensive. "Does he think he's on a wilderness safari, or what?" she muttered to herself.

"Mrs. Hammond will be right down," he growled. "I should like a cup of tea while I am waiting. Hot tea," he emphasized. "We detest tepid refreshments."

Julia went to tell Hettie to make another pot and to be sure it was as hot as she could make it. Then she returned to the parlor.

Mr. Hammond fidgeted while they waited for the pot to steep. "You should have had ample time to prepare," he complained, pulling out an ornate pocket watch and studying the time. "We allowed you more time than you asked for."

Julia bit her tongue to keep from expressing the impatient retort forming in her mind. "Yes, of course," she replied softly. "We did want to be sure that the tea was fresh—and hot, so we held back from making it."

Hettie relieved the uncomfortable situation by appearing with the fresh pot of tea. Julia poured her guest a cupful and placed it on the table near his elbow.

And he left it there until it cooled to lukewarm before taking a swallow.

When Mrs. Hammond appeared they went through the process all over again.

At last the children joined their parents. There were two girls about the same age as the twins and a boy of about five. Julia studied them. They looked snobbish, whiny, and undisciplined.

"Mama," began the oldest. "You said I wouldn't have to share a room with Miranda."

"We have already been through that," the woman argued. "I had no idea this would be such a tiny place."

Julia's indignation rose. She was about to remind the woman that the information she sent stated that the house had three bedrooms available for guests, but just then Julia's attention was averted to the boy. He had lifted the whole plateful of sandwiches and was racing across the room with them.

Julia caught her breath, sure that the child was going to dump the whole plate on her fine blue carpet, but Hettie intervened. Before the boy knew what had happened, she deftly removed the plate from his hand. He seemed about to howl in protest, when Hettie asked, "Would you like a cream puff?"

His disapproval quickly changed to delight.

"I'll serve you on the back swing," Hettie continued. "Come. I'll show you the way."

Julia breathed a relieved sigh and watched the boy and Hettie disappear.

The Hammond girls caught her attention again.

"Fredrika used all the closet and all the drawers for her things."

Julia could well imagine it. Tom had carried up more suitcases than she had been able to count.

"You must learn to share," admonished the mother. Julia guessed that the concept was totally foreign to the two girls.

"But—" began Fredrika.

"Now—no buts. We are not in a hotel, you know. We will be making do for a few days. Your papa wanted to get off to some quiet place. Away from civilization."

The look the woman gave her husband told Julia that the two were not in agreement about their destination. The man ignored his complaining wife and fussing children as he stirred cream and sugar into a second cup of hot tea.

Making do, thought Julia. *Making do—away from civilization.* Though seething, Julia maintained her composure.

"More tea, Mrs. Hammond?" she asked politely.

"The last cup was a tad cold," the woman snipped. "I do hope that shan't be the norm."

Julia went to the kitchen to make a new pot. She detested fussiness, and they were being impossible.

"I do hope that young ruffian is behaving himself in my backyard," she mumbled to herself. Just then the kitchen door burst open and Felicity entered, her eyes wide.

"Mama," she exploded, "that boy is trying to tip over the swing!"

"He's what?"

"He's trying to tip it over. He's swinging hard, and he said he's going to go so high that it flips right over."

"Oh my!" exclaimed Julia on her way to the back porch.

Tom was there by the time Julia arrived. He couldn't reason with the young boy, and he couldn't discipline the guests' child, but he could thwart his action. Tom's big, broad hand held the swing firmly so the boy, push as he might, went nowhere.

Julia thanked Tom and returned to the kitchen. Felicity and Jennifer followed her.

"How long will he be here, Mama?"

"He kicked a flower pot all across the yard."

"He ate four cream puffs all by himself."

"He says he's our boss and we are his servants."

"How long will he be here, Mama?"

Julia sighed, and her eyes pleaded for the girls to be patient.

Jennifer caught the message and nudged Felicity. Both girls fell silent.

Julia drew her two daughters close. "I didn't know that it would be this hard," she admitted. "But we must do it. We must help Papa. Do you understand?"

Both girls nodded.

"It won't be long. In fact, they are so unhappy with our accommodations that they might not even stay. It wouldn't surprise me in the least."

Seeing hope in the girls' eyes, Julia hurried on. "But we must try to keep them—to convince them. We must. Your papa—the—the other committee members—they are counting on us. Do you see? We must do the best we can—the very best—to endure."

Julia spoke the last word softly but with such determination that the girls knew how difficult the ordeal was for her. They nodded their consent.

"Can we go to our room?" asked Jennifer.

They had been told to wait on the porch in case the children needed entertaining. Julia could not ask that of them in the present circumstances. She nodded, and the girls left for the sanctuary of their room.

Oh, if only I could run and hide in my room, thought Julia, but she couldn't, so she picked up the pot of hot tea and the plate of sandwiches and returned to the parlor.

"My, it takes a long time to make a pot of tea in the wild," complained Mrs. Hammond. She refused the sandwiches, saying, "My waistline. One must not overindulge."

In spite of the difficult start, things did settle down over the next few days—or perhaps the residents of the big white house just adjusted.

Mr. Hammond was determined to make his visit a wilderness adventure. He spent most of his hours walking mountain paths pretending, Julia surmised, to be the first man who had set foot on them. To the family, he talked incessantly of his "discoveries," much to the annoyance of his wife and the boredom of his children.

The young boy, Hadley, was directed to the vacated mill site, where he spent hours running over sawdust piles and investigating the small empty buildings the mill had left behind. He roared and ran and hooted and climbed, returning home for mealtimes in a dirty, dishevelled state. But at least he was out of everyone's hair, and all those with whom he shared the house, including the Hammonds, seemed thankful for that.

Felicity and Jennifer offered friendship to Miranda and Fredrika, but the city girls turned up their noses and continued to bicker and whine. No amount of coaxing or enticing could persuade them to do otherwise, and soon the Harrigan girls gave up and left them in their own misery.

Mrs. Hammond took possession of the porch swing, demanding pillows to soften the wooden seats. Her back was bad. She had to put her feet up as well, and needed more cushions for them. Snuggled in the softness, she read penny novels and devoured so many imported chocolates that Julia figured they must have completely filled one of the mysterious suitcases. *My waistline, indeed!* thought Julia.

Along with the busy days for Julia and Hettie, John and Tom were also pressed with responsibilities. The garden needed constant care. They had a wood supply to maintain, lawns to mow, and shrubbery to trim—not only at the Harrigan house, but also at empty neighborhood homes.

In addition, Mrs. Hammond never stopped making suggestions as to how the Harrigans could make her and her family more comfortable.

"Surely, you must have attic space. If your youngsters used it, my girls could each have her own room. They are not used to being crowded together, you know."

"If this porch was screened in, it would be much more pleasant."

"The gardens would be more becoming if there were more flowers and fewer vegetables."

Julia tried to let it all pass. She ticked off each day as she left the kitchen at night. In the meantime she and Hettie devised little ways of meeting the demands.

They kept water boiling at all times. Two teapots were put into service, so there was always a hot pot at teatime.

Hettie made hearty lunches for Hadley so the whole family did not need to wait for him to return from his exploring before sitting down to dinner.

Mrs. Hammond was undisturbed on the porch swing, additional cushions borrowed from the committee members.

Men loitering in front of the train station told Mr. Hammond enough stories of bears and mountain lions to convince him that the area was truly wild and dangerous. He would have many stories to tell when he returned to the city.

And the two bickering girls—they were ignored as much as possible.

Eventually the two weeks ended, and the suitcases were repacked. Mr. Hammond took one last walk, hoping to see an elusive grizzly bear. Mrs. Hammond wriggled free of her cushions, stood up, and ate her last chocolate as she left the porch. Miranda and Fredrika whined over who would get the window seat on the return trip, and Hadley roared up and down his sawdust trail one last time before being force-cleaned for the train journey. Then they were on their way.

The whole Harrigan household breathed a sigh of relief. It was over. They had made it.

"I never would have survived without you," Julia admitted to Hettie. "I was so close to giving up."

Julia drew the payment from her apron pocket. It really wasn't much for all the work involved, but it would help—and it was a start.

"I hope the Greenwald guests are easier to manage," Hettie stated.

"Oh my! I had forgotten. They arrive tomorrow, don't they?"

Hettie nodded. The committee had decided that each

member would have a turn at keeping guests. Mrs. Green-wald was to host a young couple starting the next day.

Julia looked about her disrupted home. She was eager to restore it to its proper state. The whole place needed a good cleaning.

Hettie knew her thoughts. "We'll get to it," she assured her mistress.

"I'm sure we will," Julia stated, "but first let's have a cup of tea."

"Hot?" asked Hettie, a twinkle in her eyes.

"Very hot!" said Julia, laughing.

Chapter Eleven

New Visitors

Only Julia and three other committee members had the room and the desire to keep overnight guests. The other ladies hoped to make their living by selling goods from their craft shop. Julia was beginning to wonder if each of the four ladies would even get one turn at playing hostess.

Mrs. Greenwald's young couple quickly became bored with the small town and left before their time was up. Mrs. Clancy's first clients made other plans and did not show up at all. That meant Mrs. Clancy would have the next people on the list. Eventually an elderly couple wrote for accommodation.

Julia had received permission from four shop owners to use their facilities. The women, along with their husbands, got busy preparing the space to display merchandise. They expressed some disappointment at the meagerness of their stock as they tried to make so few items fill such big shelves.

"It will be much better next year," Julia encouraged. "We will have all winter to prepare things for the stores."

Although the women looked a bit more hopeful, Julia knew they were all wondering where they would get the funds needed to buy supplies to make the items.

"These will have to do for now," Julia continued. "It does look much better to have some of the boards off the shop windows along Main Street."

Summer was drawing to a close when two letters arrived. A family of three wanted a quiet accommodation for a two-week period and a "genteel" couple requested two rooms for an undetermined number of days. Julia hastily called a committee meeting for that afternoon.

"We don't have much time," she told the group. "Both parties plan to arrive next week."

The Adams family was next on the list, so the committee decided they would get the guests staying for the more certain period of time. Julia was given the genteel couple.

"Will you need help getting ready?" Julia asked Ruth Adams.

"Thank you, but I'm as good as ready right now. After all, I've been waiting all summer."

"Is there anything you need?" asked Julia. "Vegetables? Linens?"

"I could use some new potatoes—and perhaps a few carrots," the woman admitted.

"I'll send the girls over with some," promised Julia.

Next Julia asked for a report from the craft shop.

Matilda Pendleton shook her head. "We haven't had much business this summer. One couple bought three or four things to take home to family, and some men from the train looked in. One bought a lace collar for his wife. That's all."

It was a discouraging report but Julia tried to make the best of it.

"Well, that's a start. We're getting a good stock of summer jams and jellies now. Once word gets around, the train crews might do a lot more purchasing."

The other women didn't look too hopeful.

Julia sensed their discouragement and brought the meeting to an end. "Hettie, I think we could all use some tea," Julia prompted. As the ladies gathered around the serving table with cups of steaming tea and lemon tarts, their spirits were lifted in friendly chatter.

———

"Do you think it will be like the last time?" asked Felicity when the family gathered for family worship in the evening.

"Impossible!" John answered. "The world couldn't contain two such families." He rolled his eyes and put a horror-stricken look on his face to entertain his daughters.

Felicity laughed and Jennifer smiled at John's antics.

Julia hoped John was right but she feared that two such families just might exist. She breathed a quick prayer that she might not be called upon to endure them both in one summer.

"This will be a new family," John reminded them. "They may be 'different'—but that's what makes this venture exciting. We never are quite sure what kind of folk we will be entertaining."

"I hope they don't have a boy!" exclaimed Jennifer, remembering the last one.

"If they do, we'll need to tie down the flower pots," put in Felicity.

"And chain down the swing," added Jennifer. "And—"

"They don't have a boy," said Julia. "The next guests are just a couple."

"Old?" asked Felicity.

"I don't know. The letter just said 'genteel.' "

"What's genteel?" asked Jennifer.

"Well, that means they have good manners—good breeding. They are used to fine things," Julia explained.

Felicity rolled her eyes at her sister. "Oh-oh," she said. "The children-should-be-seen-and-not-heard kind."

John and Julia laughed.

"Well, it could be that you will need to keep down your chatter for a few days," Julia admitted, "but that shouldn't be too hard."

"I keep forgetting," said Felicity. "When I am serving in the dining room or putting fresh towels in the bath, I keep forgetting that I am not to talk—just serve."

"I know," Julia smiled. "It's difficult to shift roles, isn't it?"

John fidgeted. He hated to see his family become servants in their own home. His girls were hardly more than children and they were serving the table, doing dishes, cleaning bathrooms, and making beds. Julia had tried to assure him that the experience was good for them, but John would rather have had them learn their duties under different circumstances.

"Enough chatter for now. We all have things to do if we are to be ready for tomorrow," Julia went on. "Let's be quiet while Papa reads the Scriptures."

The girls settled themselves to listen to the scripture lesson that John had chosen for the evening reading. Then each one prayed, asking God to keep them within His will. Felicity went a step further. "Dear God," she prayed, "bring us good guests—not like the last time. Thank you that they don't have wild boys or grumpy girls. Help us to do our best to care for them and might they pay good money for all of us to live on. Amen."

———

The buggy did not carry many suitcases when Tom arrived with the guests the next afternoon. Each visitor had one small piece. Tom looked pleased as he carried the two cases to the second floor bedrooms.

"Do come in," Julia greeted the couple. "You must be weary after your long train ride. Hettie will show you your rooms and the hall bath where you may refresh yourselves. We will have tea in the main parlor in fifteen minutes."

The gentleman nodded, giving Julia a kind smile, and took his wife's arm to follow Hettie. The woman climbed the stairs with hesitation, causing Julia a moment's concern. But she completed the climb with no apparent ill effects. Julia put aside her worry and went back to the kitchen.

In fifteen minutes, just as Julia had arranged, the couple entered the parlor. They made no demands. Mr. Williams led his wife to a chair and helped her be seated. He pulled another chair up close to hers and seated himself.

"Cream and sugar?" Julia asked.

"Just sugar for me," replied the woman, "but Mr. Williams will have a bit of both."

Julia served the tea and passed the dainty sandwiches.

"My, you have a lovely home. So pretty. Not—not stark and cold like—like some places," the woman observed as she helped herself to a sandwich.

"Thank you," responded Julia. She enjoyed having her home receive proper respect.

"I love the pictures," the woman went on. "That one in the hall, of the stream and the children. I could almost taste the water the boy is offering to the girl."

Julia enjoyed the compliment. The picture was one of her favorites.

"Who is the artist?" the woman asked.

"He was an acquaintance of my father," Julia stated. "The picture was a wedding gift."

"Then I don't suppose you want to sell it?" the woman asked, her brows arched over her lifted teacup.

"No," said Julia, shaking her head. "I think not."

Julia passed the cupcakes. Mr. Williams accepted one, but Mrs. Williams politely turned down the sweets.

"I would like another cup of that lovely tea, though," she murmured. "Quite the nicest cup of tea I have had for some time."

Julia smiled. "I suspect that our cold, clear spring water has something to do with that."

"Yes," agreed the woman. "Yes, I suspect so." Then she turned to her husband. "Do you suppose we could get our water from the spring?" she asked him.

"We will drink nothing but spring water while we are here," he promised.

"I mean for our tea."

"Yes, dear. For our tea."

"But shouldn't we pay them if we are going to use their water?" she asked.

"My dear, we will pay them," he tried to assure her.

"But I didn't see you pay."

"We pay when we leave," he tried to reason.

"Are we leaving already? Goodness! It seems that we just got here," she said, rising to her feet.

Julia could not understand the strange exchange. She wondered if she should leave the room and give the man an opportunity to calm his disoriented wife.

The man stood also. "No, dear, we are not leaving yet." He eased her back into her seat. "And you are quite right," he hurried on. "We do owe this lady for her fine tea, made of fresh spring water. Here. I will pay her. See! Right now." He reached into his pocket and drew out a bill, which he handed to Julia. His wink told Julia to take the money without comment.

Julia accepted the bill with a trembling hand. "Thank you. Thank you, Mr. Williams," she managed.

Mrs. Williams settled back in her chair.

"That's better," Julia heard her say.

Mr. Williams set aside his cup. "I do think my wife needs some rest," he explained. "If you will excuse us, I will take her to her room."

Julia nodded. "Dinner will be served in the dining room at seven," she said.

Mrs. Williams allowed her husband to take her arm, help her out of her seat, and steer her toward the staircase.

"Wait!" Julia heard her say when they reached the hall. "I want to see the picture."

After several moments Julia heard the footsteps continue on.

Julia wasn't sure how to plan for dinner. Would the couple like company? Should the family join them? Or would they prefer the serenity of being alone?

During the Hammonds' visit, the twins had eaten in the kitchen and Julia and John had taken their meal in the dining room after the guests finished. But the Hammonds had been a family of five. They had almost filled the table themselves. Mr. and Mrs. Williams would not do so. Should the Harrigans join them? Julia pondered the question. She finally decided that the guests, at least for their first meal, should be served alone.

Mr. and Mrs. Williams appeared at the dining room door promptly at seven. Jennifer was given the task of serving the table. Julia oversaw the meal from the kitchen, and Felicity began clean-up at the big kitchen sink.

"She sure doesn't eat much," Jennifer said on a trip to the kitchen.

"I noticed that," replied Julia.

"Do you think she doesn't like our food?" asked Felicity.

"She keeps saying 'this is so good' and 'that is delicious,' " said Jennifer, "but she doesn't even eat it. Just takes a bite or two and lets the rest sit on her plate."

"Perhaps she doesn't have a very big appetite," Julia commented. "She does seem rather frail. Maybe she has been ill."

"He eats well," said Jennifer. "He had two helpings of everything."

"Good," Julia responded. "He is very thin. He needs to put on some weight."

Jennifer disappeared to clear the table and returned a moment later with a frown on her face.

"What's wrong?" asked Julia.

"She asked how long I have been working here. When I told her I live here, she said 'poor child' and patted my arm. Then she said she did hope it wouldn't be too long until I'd be able to leave. What did she mean, Mama?"

"I have no idea," said Julia.

"Did her husband know what she meant?" asked Felicity.

"I—I don't know. I had the feeling he was trying to—to hurry her. He suggested a walk in the garden for some fresh air. He asked me for permission. When I told him to go right ahead, she patted my arm again and said, 'Such a nice, sweet girl. I'll talk to the people in charge.' And he hurried her away."

"That's strange," said Felicity.

Julia agreed, but she said nothing to the girls.

"If they have finished eating, clear the table and reset it," she instructed Jennifer. "Felicity, go call your papa from the garden. We will have our dinner now."

Chapter Twelve

Strangers

The next morning when Julia came down the stairs, Mrs. Williams was sitting in the hall studying the painting of the quiet stream and the children.

"It is so peaceful," she murmured with a sweet smile flickering on her lips.

"Yes," agreed Julia. "Yes, it is." Julia's eyes shifted to the hall clock. "My, you are up early," she continued. "Were you unable to sleep?"

"Sleep?" asked the woman. "Oh no, I don't sleep. James sleeps. He sleeps for both of us. I don't sleep now."

"I see," said Julia. "Would you like a cup of tea or coffee while you wait for your breakfast?"

The elderly woman took on the look of a child being offered a forbidden treat. "Oh, could I?" she whispered, glancing around as if expecting someone to spoil their plan.

"Certainly," said Julia. "It will take just a few minutes. Would you like me to bring it to the parlor or into the dining room?"

"I thought you meant with you," the frail woman said with some disappointment.

Julia recovered quickly from her surprise. "If you'd like to come to the kitchen, that would be fine," she offered.

"I just love kitchens," she giggled like a schoolgirl. "So— so cozy with the fire burning."

Julia offered an arm.

"They'll never know, will they?" the elderly woman chuckled. She took Julia's arm eagerly and tottered along to the kitchen.

She is frail, Julia observed. *And confused. She must have been very ill. I must speak to the girls. We will all need to be patient and kind with her.*

Julia seated her guest in a kitchen chair at the gingham-covered table and hastened to start the morning tasks. She had just added wood to the fire when the back door opened and Hettie entered. Her eyes widened for an instant at the sight of their guest. Then she smiled and set to work on breakfast muffins.

"Mrs. Williams wanted to join us in the kitchen," Julia explained. "What would you like, Mrs. Williams? Tea or coffee?"

"Oh, I'm not allowed coffee," the woman said. "It's not good for my—for my something. I can't remember what. But I could have some this morning. You wouldn't tell them, would you?"

Hettie cast a questioning glance toward Julia, then went on stirring the muffin batter.

"Tea sounds good," mused Julia. "I think we should all have a cup just as soon as the water gets hot. Don't you agree, Hettie?"

"Right, tea sounds good to me."

Julia had no idea what the "something" might be to which Mrs. Williams was referring, but she would take no chances, just in case there was indeed a "something."

"We'll have a good cup of tea with fresh, clear spring water," Julia went on.

Mrs. Williams looked as though she had never heard of such a thing as spring water. "I—I like mine with hot water, please," she said timidly, then quickly added, "If it's not too much trouble."

"Oh no. No trouble at all," Julia assured her. "We'll certainly make it with hot water."

"And a tiny bit of cream."

Julia nodded. The woman had asked for sugar the afternoon before.

As soon as the tea was ready Julia served her guest, then
busied herself with breakfast preparations.

"Whose turn is it to set the table?" she asked Hettie.

"Felicity's," Hettie answered. "Jennifer did dining room
duty last night."

Julia nodded. She would have remembered if she had
stopped to think about it. Her mind was dwelling too heavily
on the woman at her kitchen table.

Felicity soon entered, yawning as she tied her crisp apron
over her dress.

"Good morning," piped the women. "Are you still here?"
Felicity stopped in her tracks. Her eyes traveled from the
woman to her mother and then back to the woman again.

"Yes," she said hesitantly. "I'm still here."

"Would you like some tea?" asked the woman, patting the
chair beside her.

"No—no thank you," replied Felicity. "I must set the table."

"Is it time to eat again—already? Oh my, I do hope it's
not that awful stew."

She had been served no stew at the Harrigans'.

Julia saw the merriment light up Felicity's eyes. "Felicity," she said before her daughter could think of some teasing
response, "use the blue napkins."

Felicity nodded, and Julia hoped she had averted a problem.

I must have a talk with the girls, Julia told herself. *It is
obvious that Mrs. Williams is ill. We must all be careful.*

"Mrs. Williams, would you like another cup of tea?"

Just as Julia finished her question, the door flung open
and a wild Mr. Williams burst through.

"Have you seen—?" He stopped in mid-sentence when his
eyes fell on the woman at the kitchen table. He slumped into
a nearby chair and covered his heart with his hand. "Oh,
thank goodness!" he exclaimed. "I was worried sick when I
didn't find her in her room. I—I never oversleep like this. It

must have been the long train ride or—"

"She's fine," said Julia. "Just having a cup of tea. Would you care for some?"

Mr. Williams first shook his head, but then he changed his mind. "Yes, I think I will after all." He still looked pale and shaken. Julia poured his tea and set it before him.

Mrs. Williams smiled contentedly, apparently pleased that her husband had joined them. She patted his hand. The fear was beginning to leave his eyes, but Julia noticed that his hand still trembled when he lifted the cup to his lips.

Jennifer entered the kitchen. She was wearing a green calico dress that matched her sister's. Mrs. Williams looked at her out of the corner of her eye and gave her a conspiratorial nod.

"Are you done already?" asked the woman.

"Done?" asked Jennifer.

"I think she has you confused with Felicity," Julia explained in a whisper. "Felicity was just here and is now setting the table for breakfast."

Mrs. Williams motioned for Jennifer to come closer to her. Then she laid a hand on the girl's arm. "Don't worry," she whispered. "I promised to work on it—and I will. All you will need is a disguise of some kind."

Jennifer looked at Mr. Williams for some explanation. He appeared both anguished and embarrassed. Jennifer reached down and took the frail hand in hers. "Thank you," she said simply. "You're very kind."

The door opened again and Felicity came into the kitchen. "Jen," she began, "where did you put the blue sugar and creamer?"

"On the bottom shelf of the buffet."

Felicity saw Mrs. Williams look from one twin to the other, then back again. Suddenly her face lit up in a big smile. "That is so clever!" she exclaimed. "I never would have thought of it. It's the perfect disguise. They will never catch you—when you are two. They won't know which one to chase. You'll be able to get away for sure." She clapped her hands in childish glee and laughed with uninhibited pleasure.

Mr. Williams moved to his wife. "Come," he said. "You've had enough tea. Let's take a little walk before breakfast."

He helped her up, and she went without protest. "So clever," she chuckled as she left the room. "I would never have thought of it. I wonder how she does that."

That afternoon as Julia and Hettie were preparing supper, Mr. Williams tapped on the kitchen door.

"Mrs. Harrigan—could I see you for a moment?" he began hesitantly.

Julia nodded and wiped her hands on her apron. Then she took the apron off and laid it on a kitchen chair.

"Let's go to the porch swing," she suggested, leading the way.

Julia welcomed a few moments to sit quietly in the shade, but she knew she could not relax completely. Mr. Williams had something important on his mind.

"I'm—I'm sure you have noticed that Mrs. Williams can—can get a bit confused at times," he began slowly.

Julia nodded. "She's a very pleasant person," she said to ease his anxiety.

"Yes. Yes, she is. A dear, good woman. She always has been." His eyes took on a distant look before filling with tears.

"She has not been well. Has been very sick, in fact," he explained.

"I thought as much," Julia said softly.

"I—I brought her here hoping that the—the quietness would be good for her."

"We'll do all we can to make it so," said Julia.

"All of you have been most kind," the man continued. "You—you just don't know how—how beside myself I have been. I—I hardly know how to—to care for her."

"It must be very difficult for you," Julia agreed.

"I just wanted you to know—to understand," he continued.

"Of course," said Julia. "Please, please let us know how

we can help. If there is anything you need—"

"We are very comfortable," he quickly assured Julia. Then he paused. "But there is one thing—"

Julia waited for him to go on.

"Would it—would it be possible for your good husband to put a—a lock on her door?"

Julia tried to hide her surprise.

"This morning I was so frightened. This time it was only the kitchen, but what if—what if she had wandered off down one of the mountain trails? I don't know what I would have done . . ."

Julia understood the man's concern. "Of course," she said. "John will put a lock on the door as soon as she wakes up from her nap."

"Thank you. Thank you!" the man exclaimed. "Now I must get back. She doesn't sleep well."

He hurried off, and Julia gave the swing a slight push and let the motion sweep away some of the anxiety from her heart.

"The poor soul," she said softly. "What an awful burden. I wonder how long this has been going on?"

————

The family accepted Mrs. Williams with her strangeness. Indeed, they decided to do more than accept her. They decided to try to help her.

"Do you think they like to be alone so much?" Jennifer asked at their evening prayer hour.

"I don't know. He certainly wants peace and tranquillity for her."

"But if we sat quietly, and talked quietly, do you think it might be good for her to have company at meals?"

"I will talk to Mr. Williams," Julia promised. "We'll let him decide."

"In the meantime," said John, "if she wants to sit in the hall and look at the painting—or in the kitchen to drink tea—then we'll let her."

"She *is* friendly," stated Felicity.

"And she's not bossy," added Jennifer.

"She always says 'thank you,' " Felicity recalled.

"I like her," Jennifer concluded.

"It's a shame we can't help her more," said Julia. "She seems so sweet."

"Maybe they will stay longer if they like it here and it's peaceful and quiet. Do you think so, Mama?"

"Perhaps," said Julia.

"We'll try to make her feel at home," Jennifer decided.

They included the Williams couple in their prayers that night.

————

Three days later Julia was startled by a knock at the door. Two men in dark uniforms showed Julia their credentials.

"Are you Mrs. Harrigan?" asked the larger of the two.

"That's right," Julia nodded.

"May we come in?"

Julia moved aside and motioned them in. She led the way to the parlor.

The smaller man took charge.

"Mrs. Harrigan, I understand that you keep boarders."

"Short-term guests," Julia corrected.

"Do you ask for references?" he asked.

"No."

"So your guests at present are strangers?" Without waiting for her answer he continued. "We understand that you have a Mr. Williams and his—his companion here."

"Yes."

"You know nothing about them?"

"Just that they wanted a quiet place to—for Mrs. Williams to regain her strength."

The men looked at each other.

"Are they here now?"

"Why, yes. They are—are resting."

"So you know that the woman has been ill?" asked the larger man.

"Yes. Mr. Williams said she has been ailing," admitted Julia.

"What else did he tell you?"

"Nothing."

"Then you don't know that she has been assigned to an asylum?"

Julia drew in her breath sharply.

"And that she is absent without permission? That Mr. Williams spirited her away to avoid the authorities?"

"What? I—I can't believe it. They seem like—like such a fine couple—"

"In fact," the man continued, "Mr. Williams is indeed Mr. Williams, but Mrs. Williams is Miss Margaret Whistler."

"But—why—why would—?"

"Apparently they were childhood sweethearts and then the war and circumstances separated them. When he returned she had been terribly ill, and the fever—well, she has been in the asylum for years. He kept visiting her, determined that she would recover. She didn't. He kept asking for her release, but they wouldn't grant it. Finally he just took it upon himself to run off with her."

Julia could not hide her amazement. "Mr. Williams? There must be some mistake. He seems so—so—"

"Shrewd? Oh, he's shrewd all right. Downright clever. He planned the whole escape himself. Outsmarted everybody. Folks at the hospital got so they trusted him—and then he took off. Now it is costing a small fortune to find them and take them back."

"But surely—surely you don't have to take them back. He cares for her. He seems most solicitous. He—"

"Oh yes. He cares. He means well. We've been told that he even has the foolish notion of a hasty marriage. Thinks that will give her 'security'—help her get well again. It just doesn't work. We've tried to let others out. They do all right for a few days or possibly weeks—and then they need to be locked up again."

"Locked up?" gasped Julia. It sounded so cruel. "What do you mean? She is such a—a sweet, agreeable person. Perhaps a bit confused, but perfectly harmless. She—"

"No one confined to an asylum can be considered harmless," said the man. "She might seem fine today—but who knows what her confusion will cause her to do tomorrow? She might start setting fires, or she might take a knife to someone or something."

Chapter 13

A Twist

Julia's eyes widened with shock. "Not Mrs. Williams!" she gasped.

"Miss Whistler," corrected the smaller of the two men.

"Why I—I just can't believe it. I mean—"

"We're going to be taking them back," said the bigger man.

"Oh my! I do wish—You don't think they would be fine if someone watched out for them? I mean—"

"Sorry, ma'am, but we can't take those chances."

"Of course," murmured Julia.

"Now if you'll just go get your boarders, we'll be on our way."

"House guests," Julia corrected. All the way up the long flight of stairs and down the hallway Julia mumbled. "What a shame! What an awful shame." She raised her calico apron to brush away the tears.

She hesitated before the door of the bedroom occupied by Mr. Williams. She had decided to speak to him first. He could talk to his wife—to Miss Whistler. He would know the best way to break the news to her.

Julia sniffed away her tears and lifted a trembling hand to knock. There was no answer so she knocked again. Still no answer.

"Mr. Williams? Mr. Williams," called Julia, softly at first

99

and then louder. Still no answer.

"That's funny, I didn't see them go out."

A noise behind Julia caused her to wheel around. The small man was eyeing her with suspicion.

"They . . . they don't seem to be in," Julia faltered. "I didn't see them go out, but perhaps—"

The man pushed past Julia. He opened the door without knocking and entered the room with one swift motion.

Julia peered over his shoulder. The room was empty. The bed neatly made. The two small suitcases missing.

"He's—he's gone. But how—?"

"Tricky little—" The man bit off the rest of his remark, perhaps remembering that a lady was present. Then he confronted Julia. "You really knew nothing of this?" he quizzed.

"No, I had no idea. They didn't say—I mean, he said they would stay until—"

"Well, I guess I'll just have to accept your word," he interrupted, implying that he still doubted her.

"My word can be taken," she said firmly. "God has set a standard. We are not to lie—even to protect someone—someone we have grown fond of. I tell you the truth, Mr.—Mr.—"

"Is there any place you know of where they might be?"

"No," said Julia.

"No place where they liked to go?"

"No."

"Is there any way out of this town?"

"Just the railroad."

"When did the last train go through?"

"Why, it was the one you arrived on, I believe," answered Julia.

The man looked surprised. Then he mumbled something Julia couldn't understand. She guessed they were more words he didn't want her to hear.

"Slipped out right under our noses," he growled.

Julia turned to hide the relief in her eyes. Then she noticed something on the dresser. She crossed the room and picked it up. It was a letter addressed to her.

Dear Mrs. Harrigan,

You have been most kind to Margaret and me, and I am sorry we cannot stay as long as planned.

I have left the amount we owe you in the top drawer of this dresser. I have also left what I believe is an appropriate amount for the picture from the hallway.

Julia's eyes widened, but she said nothing to the man standing behind her. She read on.

Margaret found it so restful. I could not deny her the privilege of ownership. I do hope you understand.

I have also left money for some provisions. We made a lunch for ourselves from your kitchen pantry, not wishing to bother any of the household.

Again, thank you for your kindness.

James W. Williams, Esq.

When Julia looked up she realized the man had been reading over her shoulder.

"So they stole—"

"They did not," cut in Julia. "They paid for—for everything."

The man turned and left the room without another word to Julia. The next time she heard him speak it was to his companion, who apparently had been stationed at the open door. "Let's get going" he said, "before the trail gets cold."

Julia shuddered. *Such a foolish way to talk. I think he's been reading too many cheap who-done-its.*

Julia knew she should bid her uninvited guests good-day, but she turned instead to the drawer mentioned in the letter and opened it slowly.

A neat pile of bills was tucked in one corner. Julia lifted them. Little slips of paper were bundled with the bills, held by small clips. The first one said, "Board and room, five days, two people." Julia counted the money. The payment was exact. The next one said, "Lunch payment." Julia counted again, finding that the amount was more than ample. "My! I wonder if he emptied the whole cupboard," she exclaimed. The last bundle said, "Painting." When Julia counted the money she determined that Mr. Williams had indeed been generous.

"The poor dears," she cried. "The poor, poor dears."

Julia heard stirring behind her and turned her head. Hettie stood there, her eyes filled with questions.

"Who were those men?" Hettie began. "I saw them leaving the house, waving their arms and turning the air blue with their talk. I was scared that—"

"They were from some asylum," Julia explained.

"Asylum?" Hettie gasped.

Julia nodded.

"What did they want with you?" asked Hettie, still stunned.

"No—no. Not me. Them." Julia waved a hand toward the vacant room.

"Them?" Hettie exclaimed, following Julia's gaze. "Them? Why?"

"They—they escaped."

"Escaped?"

Julia began to laugh helplessly. She waved the money at Hettie and picked up a corner of her apron to wipe her eyes.

Hettie looked at her, her face perplexed, her eyes filled with concern.

"Oh, Hettie. It's really—it's really quite funny. He outsmarted them. Again. That funny little man. Mr. Williams. He—he's as sharp as—"

Hettie was still shaking her head, wondering if Julia herself needed an asylum.

Through spurts of laughter Julia told Hettie the story. "They came here to get Mr. Williams. He had been a visitor at the asylum where Mrs. Williams—no Miss Whistler—that was her real name—was a patient. They weren't married at all. Well, Mr. Williams tried to get her discharged, but she never seemed to get well and so they kept her in the asylum. He loved her, and when they wouldn't discharge her to his keeping—well—he just stole her away. They are really—how do you say it—on the lam—the run. And those two men thought they had caught up with them here—but when I came up to call Mr. Williams—he was already gone."

Julia was laughing again, great tears rolling down her

cheeks. Hettie couldn't tell if her tears were from laughing or crying. Julia didn't know either.

"It's sort of sad," Julia stopped to say. "Sad—and sweet. Imagine—the old gentleman loving her enough to risk everything. He left only a note—and the money." Then Julia's face brightened. "Well, I'm glad," she said firmly. "I'm glad they got away. The men from the asylum implied that I knew all about this. That I helped them escape. Well, I didn't. But I'm not sure I wouldn't have—had I known."

At the sound of Hettie's gasp, Julia hastened to explain. "Well, why not? I mean, they are hurting no one. Why shouldn't they be free to live their own lives? Wouldn't it have been wonderful if we could have had the minister marry them? Just think! We could have given them a little reception!"

Hettie did not respond enthusiastically.

"Don't you think—?"

"I think they are total strangers," said Hettie slowly but firmly. "I think they were fugitives. We don't know much at all about their circumstances—but—if she was in an asylum, then there must have been a need for her to be there. A reason."

Julia sobered. Hettie was right. "Well, they seemed so—so blameless—so sweet," Julia ventured.

Hettie nodded.

"They left the money," Julia said again, showing Hettie the bundles. "He was very, very generous. He figured the cost of the rooms exactly. And he left money for the picture, the one from the hallway. The one she would sit and look at," Julia explained. "He even left money for the food they took with them."

"So that's where it went," Hettie said. "I went to get dinner and couldn't find—"

"Did they take much? He certainly left adequate payment."

"I haven't checked closely. I just couldn't find some things I was looking for. I couldn't understand—and when I saw those two strange men I started to worry."

Julia's eyes darkened as she remembered the two men. She tucked the bills in her apron pocket.

"Well, as you say, perhaps she should be back at the asylum. Perhaps there is a reason for her being there. But—well, quite frankly, I'm glad they got away. I wish them the best—wherever they are, and I hope they are able to outsmart those two bloodhounds—forever."

Julia closed the dresser drawer and wiped her hands across her apron.

"Now, perhaps we should check the pantry. We might need to do some shopping before dinner."

Chapter Fourteen

Summer's End

Julia hung a small mirror in the hall where the painting had been. She missed the quiet scene, but she would not have taken it back from the woman who had found so much joy in it. "I do hope it brings you many hours of pleasure," Julia whispered as she adjusted the mirror.

Julia went to the kitchen to help Hettie prepare tea for the committee meeting. Jennifer and Felicity were already there. Felicity was bent over a rolling pin, working on pie crust, and Jennifer was whipping the filling.

The scene startled Julia. The girls had matured so much over the past weeks that she could not get used to it. At the start of summer she had two children. As it drew to an end, she was the mother of two young ladies. Julia recalled her words to John. She had told him that helping with the household chores would be good for the girls. Now Julia wasn't sure she wanted them to grow up so quickly.

"Hettie is letting us make dessert," Felicity explained, and Julia understood that both girls considered it a privilege.

"I'm sure it will be delicious," she responded.

"It's one of Papa's favorites," said Jennifer. "Lemon."

"And we are having fried parsnips and carrots," continued Felicity, "with ham."

"He'll be pleased," Julia responded.

"We want him to know that we are doing just fine," Felicity went on. "Hettie says that—"

"Fel, you talk too much," Jennifer cut in.

Julia wondered if Hettie shared the conviction. Her eyes were masked, her lips pursed.

"Well, we *are* doing fine," Julia stated, trying to believe her own words. "The money that Mr. Williams paid us certainly helped. We'll get by."

"As soon as it snows, Tom is going hunting," said Felicity.

"Hunting?" Julia had never known Tom to be a hunter.

"Hettie says moose or elk—or even deer—is just as good as beef if you know how to cook it."

Julia made no comment, but she wondered if pantry stocks were lower than she had guessed.

"Papa and Tom are taking in some of the garden things," Felicity added. "We don't want an early frost to get any of it."

Julia nodded. They could not afford to lose anything. She decided to change the subject. "We should learn today when school will begin. Are you excited?"

Jennifer showed some interest, but Felicity just shrugged. She was enjoying her time in the kitchen.

Julia turned to the trays on the kitchen table.

"I see you are ready with tea," Julia said to Hettie.

"Just last-minute things to do. You go ahead with your meeting. The girls will bring it when you need it."

Julia looked again at her two growing daughters. Then she went to the parlor to make sure the chairs were in proper place and to greet the ladies as they came.

"Do we have any reports?" Julia asked the committee members after everyone was settled.

"There hasn't been much to report," Mrs. Clancy answered after a brief silence.

"The last family bought a few items from the shop," said Matilda Pendleton. "I have the money here." She reached into her pocket and took out three envelopes.

"Mrs. Shannon, this is for one of your doilies. Mrs. Greenwald, they took one of your stuffed toys. And Mrs. Harrigan, they bought your linen tablecloth."

Matilda distributed the envelopes. Julia felt guilty. Some of the committee members needed the funds much more than she did. They had had very little money come in over the summer. Julia wondered how they were managing to live.

"Perhaps we should put the craft sales money into a pot and divide it equally," Julia suggested.

"No," Mrs. Clancy objected, shaking her head. "That wouldn't be fair. Some folks do more work—and some folks put more money into their projects—and some folks do nicer work."

The others agreed.

Julia felt her cheeks flush. There seemed to be no way to help her neighbors. "Did everyone have a good garden?" Julia continued. "Some of us may have surplus if anyone is in need."

The ladies seemed pleased with the produce from their gardens.

"Our men are planning to go hunting as soon as the snow falls," Julia said. "Perhaps we can share wild meat—"

"Jim has been hunting already," said Maude Shannon.

So had some of the other husbands, they learned.

"Then no one is short of supplies?" Julia asked.

"Supplies, yes. Vegetables and meat, no," answered Mrs. Clancy.

"We don't have much flour or tea. Salt is getting low. Baking things are in short supply," said Mrs. Adams.

"I'll check what I have," Julia promised. "Perhaps we have a bit to spare." Heads dropped slightly. Julia knew the women were not used to charity, so she hastened to explain. "We can work out some means of exchange. Perhaps grocery items in exchange for a lace collar or linen handkerchiefs. I can put the items back into the craft shop and sell them next year."

The women brightened. That seemed fair.

"Perhaps I can make arrangements with Mr. Perry at the store. I will leave money on account, and you can make your purchases and leave the payment for me to pick up." Julia referred briefly to the notes she held in her hand. "Now, Mrs.

Clancy, have you a date regarding school opening?"

"Still no word," Mrs. Clancy answered. "I wrote—I even put through a wire—but nothing."

"Oh my," said Julia. "It is late—"

"I know, but there's nothing more I can do about it."

"Of course," Julia replied. "Thank you for doing all you could."

"I—I'm afraid I have some bad news too," announced Mrs. Wright, the pastor's wife. All eyes turned toward her.

"We—we just received word that we are to be moved to another parish."

Shocked looks, shadowed faces turned toward Mrs. Wright.

"Who will come to take your place?" asked Julia.

"That's the difficulty," said Mrs. Wright. "They won't be sending anyone. They want to—to close the church."

"Close the church? But we need the church, especially now. How can they close it?" Julia asked.

"Well, they feel the congregation is too small to—"

"But there are still eight or nine—maybe even a dozen families in town," Julia interrupted.

"Yes," agreed the woman, studying her embroidered handkerchief. "But only three families come."

It was true. Only the Adams family joined the Harrigans and Tom and Hettie at church on Sunday mornings.

"When will you leave? When will the church close?" Julia asked.

"The end of the year."

"Surely we can do something before then to make them change their minds. We've lost so much already. We can't give up our church too. What if attendance increased? Would they leave it open?"

"I—I don't know. They might."

"We need the church," Julia said again to her neighbors. "We need a minister here for the difficult times—now more than ever. We can't let the church go."

Some nodded, others looked away, unwilling to meet Julia's gaze.

"We'll see what we can do between now and the end of the year," Julia assured Mrs. Wright. Then with a trembling voice she announced tea was ready.

————

That night, after they had gone to bed, Julia told John the news.

"John, we can't let the church go. We just can't. We need it. Our children need it. The whole town needs it. What if—what if someone were to get sick or—or die?"

John nodded in agreement. "So how can we save it?"

"We have to increase the attendance."

"Jule, folks have moved, and there is still nothing to bring them back."

"I'm not talking about them," said Julia. "I'm talking about the ones who are still here. There must be thirty or so still in town. That would be enough to keep a church open, don't you think?"

"It would if they all went to church, Jule, but they don't. The church has been here for years, and so have they, and they only go on special occasions. How can we change that?"

"They need the church," Julia insisted. "More than ever, they need the church. I don't know how they ever manage to get along without it—without God. Especially now that things are so hard. How do they get by without prayer, John? What do they do when they need answers?"

John just shook his head in the darkness.

"Well, it has dawned on me that I haven't been doing my job," said Julia softly. "Here I am, trying to save their homes, their possessions, their—their way of life—and I haven't even been thinking about saving their souls."

There was silence in the room.

"What do you plan to do?" John asked at last.

"I—I don't know. I wish I knew. I need to do some praying. A lot of praying. Perhaps God will show me. Show us."

Silence again. John, too, was thinking on Julia's words.

"I don't know why I didn't realize it earlier," went on Julia. "For—for some reason I—I guess I thought that believing—going to church—trying to live right—was enough. It's not, John. Not when your neighbors don't know—don't understand about—about God."

John drew her close. "We'll pray, Jule," he said softly, "for the people who are left. Maybe there is still something we can do for them. We might not be able to help them find work, but maybe we can help them find God."

Julia nodded her head against John's chest. Tears trickled from her eyes onto his pajamas.

"I—I hope we're not too late," she whispered in the darkness.

————

Julia stopped at Mr. Perry's store the next morning. She pushed open the squeaky door and stepped inside.

"Good morning, Mrs. Harrigan," the elderly bachelor greeted her.

"Good morning, Mr. Perry."

"So how is the committee doin'?"

"We haven't had a very good summer," Julia admitted. "I hope things will improve next year." Julia let her eyes travel over the shelves. Stock was very low. She remembered when the shelves had been crowded with merchandise. Sudden fear gripped her.

"You—you wouldn't be planning to move, would you, Mr. Perry?" she asked, keeping her voice as even as she could.

Mr. Perry let his eyes travel over the shelves. He understood her concern.

"Me? Never. Not me," he hastened to explain. "I got no place else to go. This here spot is mine—bought and paid for. Don't have much laid aside—but it's enough. Don't take much for me to live on. I can order in the supplies I'm needin' and pick them up at the train. Live cheaper here than any other place I know. 'Sides," he finished softly, "I like it here."

Julia was glad to hear that.

"Just don't need to keep as much stock on the shelves no more. Folks ain't buyin' like they used to."

"Perhaps it will pick up again," Julia said, her fears relieved. She produced her money from the sale of the linen tablecloth and explained her mission. "The money won't go far—not nearly far enough, but it's the best I can do—for the present."

"Be glad to accommodate," Mr. Perry said. "Very nice of you, Mrs. Harrigan."

Julia picked up the few items she needed and left for home. She was relieved to have the matter cared for, though it had been difficult to leave behind so much of her income when her family needed it so badly.

Well, the others need it more, she told herself as she walked home in the warmth of the autumn sun. *God will supply—in plenty of time—as the need arises.*

Two days later Julia heard loud knocking at the front door. She hurried to answer, for it sounded urgent. There stood Mrs. Clancy, her face red, her chest heaving from over-exertion. Although she was out of breath, she started talking before Julia even had a chance to invite her in.

"The wire just came through," she panted. "The wire about school starting."

"Oh yes," said Julia. "Come in. Let's hear the news."

Mrs. Clancy did come in, but it was clear that she did not intend to sit down for a visit. She waved the wire beneath Julia's nose.

"Right here," she stated.

"When?" asked Julia. "When will the children be going back to school? The girls will be excited. I can hardly wait to tell them."

"See for yourself," said Mrs. Clancy, and she pushed the telegram in front of Julia for her to read.

IN REPLY STOP NO TEACHER FOR SCHOOL STOP TOO FEW PUPILS STOP

"What?" She looked at Mrs. Clancy. "What does this mean? It doesn't make any sense."

"They aren't starting school at all," said Mrs. Clancy. "They think our youngsters don't matter. We won't be having school this year. What do we do now, Mrs. Harrigan? What do we do now?"

Chapter Fifteen

Winter

John talked about sending the girls away for school, but both he and Julia knew there was no money for such a venture—important as they believed it to be.

"We'll borrow some books from the schoolhouse," Julia decided, as though it were a simple matter. "They are good students. It won't set them back to study for one year on their own. Next year we may have our school back."

John nodded. It seemed all they could do for the present.

Julia assigned daily portions for study. She spent three hours every morning going over lessons with the girls.

At first it seemed fun, even exciting, but the excitement soon wore off. Julia tried to think of ways to make the lessons interesting, but she had too many other things on her mind.

Winter came early. Julia was thankful that John and Tom had already dug the potatoes and pulled the remaining carrots. They could ill afford to have vegetables under the snow rather than in the root cellar.

On each of the first days of snow, John and Tom shouldered their rifles and took to the forested hillsides, hoping to bring home meat. Day after day they tramped through the frosted world, but each time they returned discouraged and empty-handed.

Jim Shannon was the first to have success in winter hunting. He brought a large venison roast to the Harrigans. Julia was glad for the meat. They had been dining on vegetables for a number of days.

"Portion it out, Hettie," Julia advised. "We don't know how long it will be until we get more."

Hettie followed instructions, reserving enough meat for stews and pot pies for several days.

John worked hard to build up the wood supply; then he left on an extended hunting trip. On his fourth day he returned with a yearling elk. It was an answer to prayer for Julia. But after dividing it among the townsfolk, she realized that the remaining portion would not last long.

But then Mac Pendleton got a small buck, and Jim Shannon shot another.

Julia began to relax. *With so many men hunting we are sure to have something for the stew pots,* she reasoned.

How to save the church topped Julia's list of concerns. *We need the church so people will have a chance to hear the Gospel,* she kept telling herself. She organized a ladies' afternoon meeting and sent out personal invitations for Sunday services. Then she arranged special events for the children during Sunday school.

The response was not good. Few people seemed to notice. They enjoyed her afternoon meetings, and some of them even sent their children to the Sunday school classes. But they seemed no more interested in the church than they had in the past.

"Frankly, I don't know what else to do," Julia confided to John. "Do you suppose a club program would help?"

"I'll talk to the pastor," John promised. "Perhaps he'll have some ideas."

But Pastor Wright had no ideas either. "We have tried and tried to get the people interested," he sighed. "There just doesn't seem to be any concern for spiritual things. Most folks who supported the church moved when the mill closed."

"Well, we'll just keep working—and praying," John promised. "Perhaps it's not too late."

John talked to some of the men, trying to convince them that letting the church close was as bad as having the mill shut down. But the blank stares he got in response told him the men had no idea what he was talking about. They did not understand why anyone would worry about religion when just getting food on the table consumed all their energies. They did not consider spiritual needs as important as physical needs.

Julia appealed to the women at her committee meetings, but she too received only blank stares in response to her pleas. The women didn't seem to feel that church was important.

Try as they might, John and Julia couldn't get anyone interested.

"Don't you care? Don't you even care?" Julia wanted to say, but their attitude answered the question for her.

———

The families eventually decided that the children should study together. They divided them into groups—the first three grades, the second three grades, and those above. The groups were assigned to the parents whose children formed them. The mothers took turns supervising the studies each weekday morning.

Jennifer, Felicity, and Millicent Shannon were the only members of the top group. That meant the Harrigans had to supervise four mornings each week. Julia took the heavier share because Maude Shannon had children in the other groups also. Julia chose a small back room for the class area and tried to brighten it up with books, maps, and a world globe. John moved a table into the room and placed three chairs beside it.

"I hope this works," Julia heard Felicity say to Jennifer on the first morning of school. "I'm not sure what Mama will do with Millicent."

"She'll be okay," Jennifer responded.

"She's not too bright, you know," said Felicity. "She always has trouble in school."

Julia soon discovered that Felicity's assessment was accurate. Millicent was not very smart. Julia had to give most of her time and attention to Millicent, leaving her own two to study by themselves. Millicent did make some progress with the coaching, but Julia was concerned that her own girls were not getting the help and encouragement they deserved.

When Christmas came, Matilda Pendleton suggested that everyone get together.

"We should," Julia agreed. She could well imagine that the young woman was bored with the lack of excitement in town.

"Where?" asked Mrs. Shannon. "There aren't many of us, but we still won't all fit in a house."

"What about the schoolhouse?" suggested Mrs. Clancy.

"It's boarded up," sighed Mrs. Pendleton. "The whole town is boarded up."

"We can tear off the boards easily enough. Surely they owe us something for all the years we paid our taxes."

"Do you think we should?" another lady asked.

"Why not?"

"She's right," others replied.

"We won't hurt anything," went on Mrs. Clancy. "Just take off enough boards to get in, have our dinner together, and then board it up again."

It seemed harmless, even sensible.

"Do you think we should wire for permission?" asked Julia.

"No time," replied Mrs. Greenwald. "They'd have to have a meeting to consider it and by then Christmas would be over."

"The building should belong to the town, anyway," argued Mrs. Clancy.

Julia conceded. After all, Mrs. Clancy's husband was town clerk. They should know who had rightful access to the town buildings.

So the residents of the small community met together on December 24 to celebrate Christmas. Reverend Wright offered the table grace and read the Christmas story. Though this was new to some, they didn't object. Then they shared their potluck dinner, sang a few carols, and visited until the large pot of coffee ran dry.

John and Julia walked the few blocks home through the falling snow. Behind them they could hear the laughter of Felicity and Jennifer with the younger children as they shuffled along.

"They must miss children their own age," Julia commented. Then she heard Felicity yell, "Tommy Shannon, I'll get you for that!" and squeals and laughter followed the threat.

"But they do seem to be having fun," John remarked. "Children always manage to have fun. It's too bad grownups have to take life so seriously."

There was a certain wistfulness in his voice, and Julia slipped her arm through his, hoping to drive away his sadness.

"John," she said, "we *are* doing all right, aren't we? I mean, we have enough to eat. We are together. We are making it through the first year—the worst year. Things will get better, won't they?"

John squeezed her hand, but he had no ready reply.

At the end of the year the Wrights packed their belongings, boarded the train, and left. Julia had been unable to save the church.

"I won't board up the building," Rev. Wright said firmly. "Even if there is no minister, the church must be open for the people."

Julia was thankful for that. At least she could still slip into the building for a few moments of prayer.

Julia felt heavy with sorrow as she watched the Wrights depart. The townspeople needed the Gospel. How would they hear it now that their church had been taken from them?

"Honestly, Hettie," Julia admitted later that day, "sometimes I come desperately close to giving up."

The older woman patted Julia's hand and suggested tea. It was the only cure Hettie had to offer for the world's ills.

———

Winter dragged on with cold winds blowing off the mountain peaks, threatening to freeze everything in its path. Snow fell, burying their world in harsh whiteness. But on a few days the sun shone with such brilliance that the whole valley glistened like strung jewels, and there were days when the climbing temperature made folks think spring might be early.

In February, Mac and Matilda Pendleton announced that they could no longer endure the lonely settlement. They loaded their few possessions, padlocked the door of their cottage, and climbed aboard an outgoing train.

"We just keep dwindling and dwindling," Mrs. Greenwald commented. "Soon there won't be anybody left but us and Mr. Perry."

Mr. Greenwald was in charge of the local train station. He would be needed as long as the train stopped at the town. Julia still had nightmares of the train being withdrawn. She would awaken in a sweat of terror, repeating, "No. Please, no. That is all we have left!"

Julia was not the only one who had fears about the train. "If they ever take the train, that's it! The town won't survive overnight without that train," she had often heard people say.

"Well," Julia said to Mrs. Greenwald, "we still have the train. No one has threatened to take it—yet."

"One can scarcely keep a family here with no doctor, no school, no neighbors—nothing," Mrs. Greenwald replied.

Julia would have added church to the list, but the Greenwalds did not consider the church a real loss.

Julia and John felt the urgency to do something. They needed spiritual nurturing. Their children needed biblical training. Their neighbors all needed it too, though none seemed to realize it.

"We'll just have to start our own Bible study," John decided. "We'll gather those who are interested and have our own simple service."

"Where?" asked Julia, eager to get started.

John thought for a few minutes. "Not in the church. People have shied away from church in the past. Perhaps—perhaps if we have it here, like you do the committee meetings, folks might get the notion to come."

Julia nodded, her eyes beginning to shine. "Do you really think it might work?"

"Might. We'll never know 'til we try."

The next morning after breakfast, Julia set to work writing invitations for a Bible study hour and sent Jennifer and Felicity to deliver them.

Only the Adams family and Hettie and Tom came to the first meeting. John read the Scriptures and discussed the lesson. Those who wished to pray did so, and the meeting ended.

Julia kept her initial disappointment to herself, but she didn't remain disappointed for long. As the remaining winter weeks passed, a few others began to join them for worship. Mrs. Greenwald came first. Julia wondered if she came out of boredom or curiosity. Then Mrs. Shannon came, and soon she was bringing her children. Julia decided they needed a lesson for the children, so she started a children's class. Soon the news got around and other children began coaxing their parents to allow them to attend. The class grew, and Julia assigned the younger ones to Jennifer and Felicity. Excited about being involved, the girls prepared lessons on Noah and Daniel with great care.

The group grew and interest deepened. There was actually participation—excitement. Julia and John began to pray more sincerely. Perhaps this was why God had kept them in town—to win their neighbors.

But it was hard, slow work. They prayed daily for the wisdom, the strength, the commitment to keep going. They made it through the winter. Spring came, bringing warm breezes that melted the snow. Spirits lifted. Folks began to talk of gardens. Children played in the warm sunshine. They had survived the first winter with no disasters. No serious illnesses. Surely they could make it through spring and summer with ease.

Julia began her letter writing again, promising visitors a quiet and restful vacation in the beautiful Rocky Mountains. The women laid aside their winter handwork to care for household chores. The children were given a week's break from their studies, more to give their mothers a rest than anything else. And then they settled in to prepare for another season, with renewed faith and courage.

Chapter 16

Another Chance

"We know better what to expect this year," Julia said at their first committee meeting of the tourist season.

Actually, no one had gotten much experience the year before. Each family had hosted only one vacationing family. Julia had cared for two—if she counted the little old man and woman trying to outwit the authorities.

"We will take turns as before," Julia continued. "I had the last ones, so we will move down the list. We have a number of items in our shops now. Many more than last year, so perhaps business will improve for those not taking guests."

As Julia spoke, she remembered that some of the ladies had used their merchandise to buy flour and sugar at the store. Still, there would be some revenue from the sale of goods.

"And we have the jams and jellies from last year's picking," Julia added.

"I used a few jars of mine," said Mrs. Clancy, and Mrs. Greenwald admitted that she too had dipped into her supplies.

"Fine," said Julia. "Our families come first. If we need our produce to feed them, then we must use it, that's all. We'll pray for a good berry crop this year. All our children are a year older. They will be better pickers this year than last."

Maude Shannon shifted uneasily. She was to have another child in a few months. She wouldn't be picking many berries for a while. But that wasn't what worried Julia as she looked at Maude. It was the lack of a doctor. She wondered if Maude planned to go away to have the baby. She wondered whether the Shannons had family she could stay with. And what about the five other Shannon children? The townsfolk might have to care for them for a few weeks.

Julia pushed the thoughts from her mind for the present and continued her meeting.

"We all need to plant good-sized gardens. That kept us going last winter. And it will help us feed our guests and see us through another winter as well. Is anyone short of garden space? I'm sure we could find some way to—"

"We dug our neighbor's potatoes last year," interrupted Mrs. Greenwald. "They were gone. No use letting them go to waste."

"We used our neighbor's garden too," admitted Mrs. Adams, blushing.

Julia had not thought about the gardens of those who had moved away. It was only common sense that someone should benefit from the produce.

"Perhaps," she said, choosing her words carefully, "it would be wise to plant those gardens again." Julia paused, then went on. "It would keep them free of weeds, make the yards look more presentable for our summer guests, and give each of us additional garden space."

As she spoke, she wondered if it was wrong to use the neighbors' yards without permission. *Lord, show me if this is wrong. I don't want to encourage anything that displeases you,* Julia prayed silently.

"We can't care for them all," stated Mrs. Clancy, "so I suggest we use the closest and the best."

"Jim is willing to use that old tractor left behind by the mill to work up the land," said Maude Shannon. "He's already been talking about it."

Julia tried to mask her surprise, then reasoned, *This is a case of survival. Perhaps we should take advantage of every-*

thing at our disposal. If we save the town, if our venture is successful, then those who left will be able to return to their homes, their gardens.

"We must set some guidelines," Julia voiced tactfully. "I think we should call a meeting with our husbands to draw up some plans as to what is proper—and what is—is stepping over boundaries."

"Like?" said Mrs. Clancy.

"Well, like, we can plant and care for garden plots—it will be better if the yards are cared for. But if we use a garden, we must also pull the weeds. And if the owners return, the garden spot, along with its produce, belongs to them. And we can use things that have been deliberately left behind, having no value to the owner, such as the old tractor. But we must be careful not to take possession of other people's property or gain from their losses."

Julia hoped she had made a point. She would suggest to John that he call a meeting of all town residents before they ran into a serious problem of "borrowing" items left behind by vacating neighbors.

————

The new Shannon baby arrived. Mrs. Greenwald helped with the delivery in the absence of a doctor, but it was Jim Shannon who kept calm and cared for the mother and child. The baby boy was fine, and the entire settlement breathed a sigh of relief. Many prayers went up, thanking God for the child's safe arrival—even from lips that wouldn't normally have admitted to prayer. The neighborhood ladies organized help for the family for the first few weeks. Then life returned once again to its familiar routine.

————

The first paying guests arrived in July. The next came a week later. Both families spent a few dollars in the shops along Main Street.

The next guests didn't come until mid-August. Julia did not get her first turn until near the end of the month when a young couple came to take advantage of the quietness of the mountain village.

"We wanted a place where we could just be by ourselves," the young woman confided.

"We will see that you have all the time alone you desire," Julia promised her.

The Harrigans ate meals in the kitchen while the young couple was served in the dining room. Jennifer and Felicity took turns serving.

"It is so romantic," Felicity crooned the first night. "Just the two of them, with the candles and the silver. Mama, do you think they would like us to move in the Victrola so they can listen to soft music?"

Julia smiled at her romantic fourteen-year-old. "Perhaps," she said. "Why don't you ask them?"

The couple turned down Felicity's offer of dinner music. "We really don't care to linger," the young man explained.

The couple spent their first few days wandering town streets and mountain trails. Then he went for walks alone and she sat on the back porch swing, whiling away the hours with no handwork, no reading, nothing to keep herself entertained. To Julia she looked very bored, very listless, and very lonely.

"Would you like something to read?" Julia asked. "We have a number of good books on the library shelves and you are welcome to borrow them."

The young woman smiled and shook her head.

"Are you tired of walking?" Julia questioned.

"I've already seen everything there is to see."

Julia nodded. It didn't take long to see everything.

"Your husband likes to walk?"

The woman shrugged. "I guess so."

"Would you like to join us in the kitchen? We're making blueberry jam today. The girls have just returned with full pails of wild berries. Perhaps—"

"I don't think so—thank you," the young woman responded.

Julia had run out of ideas, so she left the girl alone.

Jennifer served the table that evening. "I don't think Mr. and Mrs. Alberts are very happy," she said as she brought the empty soup dishes into the kitchen and prepared to serve the main course.

"Why do you say that?" asked Julia, turning to look at her.

"They haven't said a word to each other all evening," Jennifer explained. "They just glare at each other or look at their plates. They aren't even eating much—and he is usually ravenous."

The next day Julia sent Jennifer and Felicity off to the berry patch. The young woman was on the porch swing alone again, and Julia approached her, tea tray in hand.

"Anna, I thought you might like some tea," she ventured.

The young woman didn't answer.

"It is such a beautiful day," Julia continued. "I love it when the breeze is just strong enough to stir my hair and bring the scent of flowers."

Still no response.

Julia set down the tea things and poured a cup. "Have you been married long?"

"Almost a year."

"Well, you hardly get to know each other in a year. I remember when we had been married for just a year. I was wonderfully happy. I was deeply in love with John. Still, I wasn't sure if John really knew me. Really understood me," Julia sighed. "It's funny, I wasn't even sure at times if he really loved me.

"There is so much to learn about each other," Julia went on, passing the sugar and cream. "It takes far more than a year to get in step with one's mate."

Julia offered the young woman a piece of shortcake.

"John is a good man. A wonderful man. But at first—well, I guess we didn't know how to express our love. Or else we just forgot to. I learned something then. I learned that it is basically up to the woman to set the tone for openness and closeness. We just understand a bit more about expressing love, I guess. Boys are taught not to show emotion—to be masculine. I'm not saying that's right—it's just how it is.

"Well, women don't have that problem. We are free to say how we feel. To show others we love them—by doing little things, saying little things. Women can find lots of different ways to say 'I love you.'"

Julia paused to think a moment. Then she went on. "Sometimes I feel sorry for men. We teach them one thing—and then expect quite another."

Julia sighed and stirred her tea.

"You know, I was secretly hoping that I would have a son. I wanted to—well, to break the rules. To raise a boy free to express love and tenderness. I don't mean I'd want him to be a sissy. It takes a strong man to be tender. John is that, but he still has a hard time expressing it. He just—he just holds me—comforts me—but he can't seem to say how he really feels. If I didn't know him so well, I wouldn't understand."

Julia raised her cup and sipped.

"But I didn't have a son. I had twin girls—and how I thank God for them. John and I wanted more children, but, well, God knows best. I am blessed indeed. Two girls—and a wonderful husband."

Julia fell silent, allowing the young woman some time to ponder.

At length Anna raised her head and looked into Julia's eyes. "You know, don't you? That something is—is wrong between—" She could not go on. Her eyes filled with tears and her head lowered. She bit a quivering lip between even white teeth.

"I guessed," said Julia softly. "Would you like to talk about it?"

"It's just—just—well, it isn't what I expected it to be," the young woman finished with a burst of tears.

"It never is," responded Julia.

Anna's head came up. She looked surprised.

"We expect romance, flowers, love songs," said Julia; "instead, we get dirty dishes, laundry, and silence."

"But I thought—"

"And he thought," said Julia. "I suppose he expected

things like welcome-home kisses, favorite pie, and slippers. Instead, he got broken plumbing, mounting bills, and complaints."

Anna dug for a handkerchief.

"If only there were some way to prepare for reality rather than romance," Julia went on, "marriage would have a much better chance."

"Are you saying there is no romance?"

"Oh my, no! There is romance. Our problem is that we want it *all* to be romance. And we want fulfillment—a perfect relationship—immediately. In reality we must first know each other, learn from each other, protect and support each other. We must build together. Work together. Marriage is hard work. The hardest task we will likely ever undertake. And then when we are well on the way to accomplishing some of those things—then we experience the real romance—the excitement of fulfillment and shared love. More exciting than we ever dreamed."

Julia's face was shining as she spoke the words.

That's how it had been for her and John. She loved him more—was more sure of his love for her—at the present than at any other time in their marriage, and they had enjoyed many good years together.

"I guess I thought—I guess I wanted it all—romance, fulfillment—right from the start," Anna said. "Why—why can't it be that way? I mean—I loved him—"

"And I'm sure he loved you. *Loves* you. But it takes time to work through the sharing of that love—to figure out how love works."

Julia leaned from the swing and plucked a flower from the nearby bush.

"See this rosebud?" She held it out to Anna. "It's perfect. So new, so full of promise and color. Someday it will be a full flower. Beautiful, fragrant. But just suppose I want it that way now. So I take the petals and force them to open up, to be mature—now. What will happen?"

Anna waited.

"I'd spoil it," Julia said. "I would crush and bruise it, and it would just wilt and die. It takes time to reach full-flower," Julia continued. "We must nurture it, not rush it. It will happen if we are patient—and loving."

The young woman blinked away her remaining tears.

"Here," said Julia, handing the rose to Anna, "there is a vase in the hall for it. Place the rose in your room and give it care. Watch it unfold—slowly—naturally—fully."

She patted the young girl's shoulder and moved to gather up the tea things.

Anna smiled. "Thank you," she whispered. "I—I will try. To be patient—and loving. I promise."

"That's all we can do," responded Julia. "Try. Try with all our might." She walked away with a prayer that the young man might also be willing to try.

Chapter Seventeen

Heavy Thoughts

John was not sleeping well. His mind was troubled in spite of his faith in his God, in his Jule. Things were not going as planned. The summer had turned to fall and they'd had only one paying customer. All of the reserve money was gone.

The garden had been good again. John breathed a prayer of thanks for that. But even so, they needed many items that the garden could not produce. John wondered how they would manage to purchase them.

There was also the matter of the girls' education. Another school year was drawing near. The girls needed more than Jule could teach them in home lessons. They were quickly becoming young women, and John and Julia wanted them to have a proper education—perhaps college if they were interested.

John shifted under the blankets, unable to find a comfortable position. Beside him, Julia breathed evenly. He was glad he wasn't keeping her awake with his tossing.

Oh, God, he prayed silently as he had many times before, *show me what to do. Please, show me what to do. It would break Jule's heart to leave here—this house. I could never offer her a house like this again. But we can't go on living like this—no income to speak of—nor much hope of any—and so many needs for the family.*

Help me, too, when I talk to Jule about our future. Give me the right words. Oh, God! I need you so much!

John lay in the darkness thinking about their circumstances. Perhaps he could find work at another mill. His old boss had written him on a number of occasions urging him to leave Calder Springs and join him at the new mill site. Perhaps some position would still be open—though John was sure they had found a foreman by now. Still—any job would be better than no job.

John rolled onto his back and stared at the ceiling. *The moon must be bright tonight,* he mused. Then he thought about how easily his mind slipped to other things. He let his gaze go to the window. Light sifted in around the edges of the full velvet drapes. He was tempted to rise from bed and take a stroll outside to see the mountain valley by full moonlight.

It must be pretty out there tonight, he thought. The cry of some night creature interrupted his thoughts. It was followed by the hoot of an owl. John visualized the scene. The owl, hungry and in need of food for its growing family. The small nighttime animal being caught off guard. The speed of the owl, as with one silent and powerful swoop it split the air, grasped the victim with outstretched talons, and, hardly slowing its speed, continued on to its nest.

Tonight John's empathy was with the owl. He knew the desperation of trying to provide for a family.

"We do what we have to do," he muttered.

Julia stirred. John wanted to reach out and take her in his arms—not for her comfort, but for his. But he did not want to wake her. She too was carrying a heavy burden and needed her rest. John turned so he could watch her in the moonlight, and his thoughts began to mellow.

It's a marvel we have made it this far—and with no debts. I don't know how she does it. Keeps food on the table—and the girls cared for.

Then John remembered noticing the girls at the supper table that evening. Their dresses were getting tight and short. Julia had let out all the seams and let down all the hems. There was no more room for growth—but the girls kept growing.

"They will soon be done with their growing," Julia had assured him with a careful little laugh. "They are as tall as I am now. Girls don't grow much after they reach their age."

John hoped Julia was right. She had no more bolts of material in the upstairs sewing room from which to sew new dresses.

The clock in the downstairs hall chimed three o'clock. John changed his position once more. He had to get some sleep. But sleep wouldn't come. *It's no use,* he finally sighed. *I might as well do something useful.*

John slipped out of bed and headed downstairs. The moon bathed the hallway and the stairs with enough light for him to find his way. He went first to the kitchen for a drink and then to his desk in the library.

He drew out a sheet of writing paper, dipped his pen in the ink well, and began a letter to his former boss. He would tell Jule his thoughts at the first opportunity.

———

"Look!" cried Felicity, as they dressed the next morning. Jennifer looked, though she didn't seem too concerned.

"Look how tight this bodice is getting. I feel so—so conspicuous in it. Doesn't it bother you?"

Jennifer nodded. Ill-fitting dresses bothered her too. But she didn't see any sense in fussing about them. There was really nothing her folks could do.

"Jen, do you really think Mama is going to make it?"

"What do you mean?" asked Jennifer, hoping she wouldn't need to answer the question.

"Do you really think this will ever be a resort town?"

"I don't know," answered Jennifer. "Mama has worked awfully hard to make it one."

"I know, but some things are impossible—even for Mama."

Jennifer smiled. It was one of their shared jokes. They never spoke of it to any other person. That would have been disrespectful. But through the years, they had joked with each other about their mother's need to fix things. "Let Mama do it," they would tease. "Just give it to Mama," "Bet Mama could fix it," and "Have you shown it to Mama?" as though there was not a thing in the world Julia couldn't manage, either by coaxing or by coercion.

"Well, we mustn't give up yet," whispered Jennifer. "Mama hasn't."

Felicity shrugged. "I think some of the other ladies have almost given up. Did you see Mrs. Shannon yesterday?"

Jennifer nodded. She had noticed the strained, hopeless look in the woman's face.

"Maybe she was just tired. She has so many children to care for—she must feel like the old woman in the shoe."

Felicity tied the bow at the waist of her dress. She had already forgotten about Mrs. Shannon. She studied herself in the mirror. "You know," she said to her twin, "I get more and more thankful for big aprons."

Jennifer laughed. Hettie's big aprons worked well to hide one's appearance, but they were not very becoming to young figures.

"We'd better get down to breakfast," Jennifer said with a quick glance at the clock. "Mama will be calling us if we don't hurry."

———

The day's mail brought a letter. The Harrigans were to have more house guests. Julia breathed prayers of thanks all the way home from the post office.

"We needed this one so badly, Lord," she explained. Then added, "But of course you knew that. Thank you, Lord. Thank you."

She hurried home to share her good news. "Hettie," she cried as soon as she entered the hall. "Hettie, good news. We have another family coming. A couple with two grown daughters. Next week. We only have a couple days to pre-pare."

Hettie appeared, wiping her hands on her apron. Julia had to repeat her words.

Felicity and Jennifer were called from the garden to hear the good news. John and Tom were off hauling more firewood so they would have to wait to find out.

"When are they coming?" asked Felicity.

"Monday," replied Julia, her eyes aglow.

"How long will they stay?" asked Jennifer.

"They are a bit undecided. They may stay for two weeks or more—if they like it here."

Felicity and Jennifer exchanged glances. They loved Calder Springs, but it didn't have much to offer folks who were used to excitement.

"We must get ready. Hettie, check the pantry. We'll have to make a trip to Mr. Perry's store and buy what we need on credit."

Then Julia had another thought. "Let's plan the daily menus, Hettie, and only purchase for one day at a time— that way if they leave sooner than expected—" Julia left the sentence unfinished. There was no sense in purchasing supplies and then ending up with no income to pay for them.

Hettie smiled at Julia's burst of energy. She was glad they were to have guests, but she still secretly wondered how long they could hang on.

"How far did you get with the weeding?" Julia asked the girls.

"There aren't many weeds," Felicity replied. "We have been over that garden so often this summer."

"Then let the rest go. I want you to freshen the three guest rooms. Open the windows wide and turn back the bedding. Do the floors and the dusting and clean the bathroom."

Felicity was tempted to remind her mother that they had been through the procedure enough times to know what to do, but she held her tongue. Julia was excited. She had to vent her emotions by taking charge.

The girls turned to do as bidden, Felicity chattering to Jennifer as they left.

"I think I'll run down and tell John," Julia said to Hettie

as she followed her to the kitchen. She removed her uptown slippers and put on the gardening shoes from behind the door. Then she reached for her gardening bonnet and hurried off.

"John! John!" called Julia as soon as she was within earshot. John spun around, afraid something was wrong at home.

Julia quickly dispelled his fears. "Good news," she called, waving the white envelope.

John walked toward his wife, brushing the sawdust and bits of clinging bark from his shirt as he moved.

"A letter," called Julia. "We are having more guests."

She was so excited that John decided to say nothing to dampen her spirit. He knew, however, that it would take many more guests to meet the family's growing needs. He forced a smile. "When?" he asked.

"Monday!" exclaimed Julia. She was out of breath from hurrying.

"Here, sit down," John urged her, indicating a fallen log. "Catch your breath—then tell me all about it."

Julia sat—but she did not wait to catch her breath.

"Next Monday," she hurried on. "A couple—and two girls—grown girls. They plan on a couple of weeks—but may stay much longer—if they like it. They'll like it. It's so—so beautiful here." Julia let her eyes travel over the scene before her. She gazed at the sweeping valley with the silver curve of the river, the shimmer of the distant lake, the slopes of nearby mountains rising up to join rugged crags and rocky peaks still covered by glacial ice.

John smiled. Jule did love her mountains.

"That's great!" he responded, trying to make his emotions match his words.

"Isn't it? I've been praying and praying—and here is our answer. Oh, John. This—this venture has been so difficult at times—but it has been a time of—of growing too. I have been shown over and over how God answers prayer. He never lets us down, John. Just when I think we can't make it any more, He answers my prayer again. And—He's never late. Though at times I think He's going to be."

Julia's eyes glistened. John turned away to gaze at the distant peaks. His eyes were threatening to spill over as well, but for a different reason. *Oh, God,* he prayed silently, *I wish I had Jule's faith.* His arm tightened around his wife's shoulders.

"Well, I must run," Julia said suddenly, standing swiftly to her feet. "I just wanted you to know about the letter. I left Hettie busy in the kitchen so I'd better get back and lend her a hand."

"Don't travel back as fast as you traveled out," John cautioned.

"Promise," she whispered. She gave John's hand a squeeze and started up the path that led home.

Chapter Eighteen

Sunday

A dozen or more were now meeting for weekly worship. John and Julia had talked about moving the group to the church but feared some might drop out if they did. It was less formal—less threatening perhaps—to have the Bible study in the comfort of the Harrigan parlor with coffee and scones served afterward.

Julia had a hard time keeping her thoughts on the lesson John had prepared. They kept shifting to the house guests who would be arriving on the morrow. She needed to tell the neighbors her news, but she wasn't sure how or where to begin. She must not let them see her excitement. They too needed additional funds to get through another winter. Julia did not want to gloat over her good fortune when their needs were still unmet.

Yet she must speak of it. No stranger got off the train without the whole community knowing of it. It would not do for the Blakeneys to arrive without the townspeople knowing ahead of time. Besides, Tom would need to borrow the Clancy's buggy.

Julia shifted in her seat and forced her attention back on the lesson.

Forgive me, Lord, she apologized. *But I am so troubled about this, even though I know I shouldn't be. Though I might not know how to say what I need to say, I know you will help me when the time comes.*

"What do you think Jesus meant by these words?" John was asking the group. Julia flushed, having no idea what words her husband was referring to.

I do hope he doesn't call on me! she thought.

Julia was relieved when Mrs. Adams spoke.

"I've been sittin' here, puzzling over them," she admitted. "But perhaps He means, what we try to keep—try to hang on to—can still slip from us. What we honestly, openly, give to Him, He somehow keeps for us—and might even one day allow us to have back."

"Isn't He talking about our lives too?" added Mr. Adams. "If we refuse to give our life to Him, try to hang on to it for our own pleasures and self-seeking, we will eventually lose it. We will have no future with Him in heaven. If we give our life to Him, He cares for us in the way that only He can, and will also reward us with eternal life."

"I think you are both right," said Mrs. Shannon. "He's talking about our lives—but the same principle applies to other things too. We can never hold tight to anything. We haven't the strength—nor the power to keep it. Nothing—nothing in this life is safe from destruction and decay. Take our town here—our jobs. Even our lives. We can't save anything by our determination—no matter how we try."

A feeling of doom was seeping into the room. Julia could feel it. Could sense the fear—the anxiety. She was about to speak when Tom, in his slow, drawling voice came to the rescue.

"But does it matter? I mean—I love this town. I've lived most of my life here. But life goes on. Change isn't always bad. Sometimes change is for our good. Sure, it might sadden us for a time, but if He is in charge—if we really let Him take charge—does it really matter? He is with us wherever we go."

Julia shifted again. Tom was right. They musn't fret so. They must develop more faith in the leading of God.

"But how do we know?" asked Mrs. Adams. "How do we

know when to trust—to hang on—and when to let go—to move on? I mean, I have prayed and prayed and still don't know what God wants us to do."

Julia looked around the group. She could sense that John didn't want to be the one to answer, and *she* certainly didn't feel prepared. She was still struggling with the question herself.

It was Hettie who spoke. "Don't you think," she said slowly, feeling her way, "that as long as one doesn't feel—well, compelled to move on, that it isn't time yet? I mean, don't you think we'll know when it's time—if He decides that we should?" Hettie stopped and fiddled with the worn Bible in her lap. "I'm no speaker—you all know that. I never can say what I want to say, but it seems to me—if we are truly committed to Him—He'll tell us when to stay put . . . and when to move on."

"But what if you sorta feel that it's time to be movin'?" asked Mrs. Adams.

Julia felt that she must speak. She cleared her throat and looked directly at the woman across from her. "Then—you must," she said softly. "If you feel that God is urging you—no matter how gently—then you must follow."

"My Victor has been offered a job," Mrs. Adams said in little more than a whisper. Victor stirred restlessly in his chair beside her.

"We didn't want to—to desert the—the rest of you."

"You won't be," John assured the couple. "We would never want to hold you back. If you believe this is God's answer—for you—if He is providing for your family in this way—then you must go—with our blessing."

Mr. and Mrs. Adams exchanged glances, both looking relieved.

"And that goes for all of you," said Julia. "We have banded together to try to help one another—but if any of you feel you must move from Calder Springs—then please—please don't stay here for the sake of the rest of us. We must all be free to do our own choosing." There were somber nods and somber faces all around her. Silence ruled for several minutes.

After a while Mrs. Greenwald spoke. "Mr. and Mrs. Adams have been church people for years," she reminded the group. "They know when God speaks. But what about the rest of us? Like me and—well, I won't mention any other names, but how do we know when God speaks, when we have never asked for, never looked for, His leading?"

The stillness hung heavy in the room. "I wouldn't have known—a few years ago," said Victor Adams. "A person needs to walk with God, to pray and read the Word, before he can know when God speaks and where He is leading. You might need to take that important first step toward God—accept Him as Savior—before you can hear Him speak to you, Mrs. Greenwald."

Mrs. Greenwald nodded in assent.

John was quick to seize the opportunity. "Would you like to come into the east parlor?" he asked. "We will show you how you can take that first step—to become a child of God."

She nodded again, her eyes misting.

"Victor and Ruth, will you join me?" John invited. "Julia, do you want to come?"

Julia decided to look after her other guests. After all, what if someone else expressed an interest in taking the same step of faith? "I had better stay here," she whispered to John.

Hettie and Tom went to get the coffee and scones. Julia addressed the remaining congregation. "We will all miss Victor and Ruth when they leave us," she began. "I don't know when they are planning to go—but maybe we can have a potluck dinner for them before they do. I am going to be quite busy this week. I just received a letter, and I have guests coming in—for a few days at least. The length of their stay is still indefinite. But I am sure I could find time to bid our dear friends goodbye.

"And I did mean every word of what I said a few minutes ago," she continued. "We want the best for each family here. If that means a move elsewhere—then we—you must be free to go. School should be starting, and we have no school for our children again. I don't know how much we can teach them. So all of you—do what you can, what you must. Those of us who remain behind, we understand."

Hettie set down the cups and saucers, and Tom placed the large coffee pot on the table beside them. Julia nodded to Felicity and Jennifer to start serving. Soon the room was a hum of chatter. Julia slipped out to the parlor to join John and the others.

She was met by a glowing Mrs. Greenwald, who dabbed at tears with a white lace-edged handkerchief.

"I've wanted to do that for a long time," she admitted, "but I didn't know how to go about it. And I was scared to death to go to the parson. I was afraid he would want an account of every sin I ever committed and there are—were—so many of them."

Julia knew that their former pastor would have demanded no such thing, but folks often had funny ideas about preachers.

"I had no idea that I could go directly to God—in Jesus' name—and ask forgiveness," the woman went on.

"That's how we each must do it," said Julia, giving her a warm embrace.

"Well, it's a big relief, I'll tell you that." Mrs. Greenwald turned to give Mrs. Adams a hug as well.

They rejoined the group in the main parlor. Julia noticed people watching Mrs. Greenwald. Folks were curious as to what had happened and if it had really "worked." If Mrs. Greenwald was conscious of the attention, she did not let on. She hugged each of her children, then turned to greet her neighbors with a shining face.

"I don't know why I didn't do this years ago," she told them, and they could see the new strength in her face.

———

"Oh, what a wonderful day," Julia said to the family at dinner. "Imagine! Mrs. Greenwald is the first convert of our worship services. I don't think she ever would have gone to church. Here I was praying to keep the church open, and there she was with a hungry heart but too stubborn—or afraid—to go to the services. God knew what He was doing all the time in closing the doors of the church."

"But, Mama," spoke Felicity, "what if there are others who would go to church, but won't come here?"

"I—really don't know," Julia admitted. "Maybe I said it all wrong. Maybe God didn't speak to Mrs. Greenwald *because* the church closed its doors. Maybe He had to use our group because the church *had* closed. Maybe that was the only way He could get our—my—attention. Suddenly I realized that I had an obligation. Before, I had left it all to the church. To the minister. I shouldn't have. If I had been as concerned when the church was still here as I am now—well, the church might still be open."

It was a sobering thought for Julia. She knew she had failed in her Christian commitment. She had waited too long to express concern for her neighbors.

"Well, we still have a big job to do. There are those in town who might move any day—so our time may be short. We need to share our faith with them—as God gives us opportunity."

"Jen talked to Millicent," Felicity announced.

Julia's head came up. "I didn't know that."

"She had a whole bunch of questions," said Jennifer. "I tried to explain to her—what it means to serve God."

"She's scared," continued Felicity. "Says she doesn't want to go to hell when she dies."

"Did you—do you need some help with your answers?" John asked Jennifer.

"I—I'm not sure she understood all I said. I told her that God doesn't want anyone to go to hell—that's why He sent His Son Jesus to die on the cross. Then I tried to explain how we confess the bad things—the sin—and ask Him to forgive us—then thank God for sending Jesus. Then we ask God to accept us as His children and help us live the way He wants us to—by faith."

"It sounds as if you did a good job of explaining it," said John, pleased with Jennifer.

"She said she wanted to think about it some more," went on Jennifer.

"She should think about it carefully," John agreed. "It is not a decision to be made lightly."

John pushed back from the table. "I don't think we should wait until our family worship time to remember these people in prayer. Let's stop and pray for them right now."

Each person at the table said a brief prayer for Mrs. Greenwald, that God would help her grow in her knowledge and understanding of Him, and for Millicent, that she might understand the meaning of the step she was considering, and that she might make the right choice.

Chapter Nineteen

The Blakeneys

On Monday morning Julia tried to get her mind back on preparations for her coming house guests, but her thoughts insisted on returning to the previous day. The eternal significance of Sunday's events made the coming of visitors much less important to Julia. She prayed that Mrs. Greenwald's decision would be strengthened as days passed, and that Millicent too would come to understand the importance of the decision she was considering and be bold enough to make it. She also prayed that Jennifer would have the wisdom to answer Millicent's questions.

Julia made one last round of the house to check that all was in readiness. She placed fresh fall flowers in the bedrooms and on tables throughout the main floor and sent Tom off to the station to meet the train.

Julia's heart pounded as she awaited her new guests. To help ease her tension she went to the kitchen to see Hettie. *Perhaps a chat, a cup of tea, or both, will calm my nerves,* she thought.

"Is the kettle hot, Hettie?" she asked as she entered the room with a swish of her skirts.

"Sure is." Hettie moved to get the teapot and the cups. She could sense that Julia was agitated. It was not a usual thing.

"Are the girls around?" asked Julia.

"I sent them to the store for the things I'll need for the guests," answered Hettie.

Julia took a seat at the kitchen table.

"Did they open the windows to let fresh air into the bedrooms?" she asked, though why she asked she didn't know. She had seen the curtains stirring in the light breeze when she made her last check of the rooms.

Hettie nodded. She too knew that Julia had just checked the rooms.

"Why do I feel so nervous?" Julia asked. "It's not as if this is our first experience with guests."

"They're likely the last guests of the season," Hettie answered. "We need the money badly."

Hettie was right. It seemed reason enough for a case of the jitters.

Hettie set the tea cup in front of Julia and asked, "You want cake or cookies?"

"Yes, please," Julia surprised Hettie by saying. Julia never took sweets with her tea, saying it was not good to have too much sugar.

"Which?" asked Hettie, and Julia looked puzzled by the question.

"Cookies or cake?" repeated Hettie.

Julia shrugged her shoulders, and Hettie placed some sugar cookies on a plate.

"I will need to be at the door to greet them," Julia murmured.

"No hurry. We'll hear the whistle long before they arrive."

Julia took a cookie from the plate. "There seems to be so much to think about all the time that my head fairly swims," she admitted.

"Like?" prompted Hettie.

"The girls mostly, I guess," answered Julia. "Some days I wonder if this is fair to them. I said to John once that learning household chores would be good for them—and it is. But shouldn't they have a chance to learn other things too?

"I think of my own youth," Julia continued. "It was so

different. I took lessons in piano, tennis, riding, French. I went to a fine finishing school. My girls won't know much more than how to scrub floors, make beds, bake cookies, and hoe gardens. Is that enough, Hettie?"

"They still have time," Hettie comforted.

"Do you think—?"

The train whistle blew before Julia finished her sentence, and she forgot her question, her tea, and her half-eaten cookie.

"They're here!" she said excitedly. She rose quickly from her chair.

"No. No, it'll take Tom a bit of time to get them here. The train is just pulling in."

Julia brushed her skirts, lifted trembling hands to her hair, and sat down again. But she couldn't stay still for long. After one more sip of tea she left the kitchen for a final check of the house.

————

"Is this all there is to your town?" Mr. Blakeney asked Tom as the horses trotted along Main Street.

Tom hardly knew how to answer. If the Blakeneys expected a hustling, bustling town, they had not read the brochure carefully.

Tom cleared his throat to answer, but Mrs. Blakeney cut in. "It is just what we wanted, isn't it, Thaddeus?" Her shrill voice made the words into a command rather than an observation.

The man only sniffed.

The two younger women stared directly ahead, no questions on their lips or in their eyes, no apparent interest in the town at all.

They passed the yard where the Shannon children played. As the team approached, the game stopped and four pairs of curious eyes looked at the passengers in the buggy. One lifted a pudgy hand to wave, and Tom dipped his head in reply.

"I do hope we won't be harassed by curious neighbors," said the older woman.

Tom noted all of the boarded-up houses. It was obvious they were empty. Not much harassment from neighbors there.

Julia was waiting at the door, Hettie close behind her. Mr. Blakeney bowed stiffly, but his wife was too busy looking around to notice Julia's welcome. She studied all she saw.

"It should do just fine," Julia heard her say to her husband. When at last she turned to Julia, she gave an order. "Show us to our rooms." Then to Hettie she said, "You will draw a bath for Miss Priscilla at once. She is very weary from the journey."

She turned then to Tom. "The suitcases will be needed immediately. I will point out to you which ones go in which rooms."

Julia, who normally sent Hettie up with the guests, led the party up the stairs herself. She indicated the three available rooms with the shared bath in the hallway. Hettie was already in the bathroom filling the tub.

"Priscilla, you may choose," the older woman said to one of her daughters.

The girl surveyed each room, then looked them over a second time, studied them more closely a third time, and finally settled on the room that overlooked the valley.

"Your father and I will take the room across the hall," Mrs. Blakeney informed the young woman. The third room was thus assigned to the second daughter, who moved into it without a word.

"Tea will be served in the main parlor in half an hour," Julia told her guests.

"So long?" asked the woman.

"I—I thought we must allow your daughter time to properly enjoy her bath," Julia explained.

"She will have tea in her room," Mrs. Blakeney replied. "The rest of us will be ready in ten minutes."

"As you wish," Julia answered. *No wonder I have been*

nervous about these guests, she thought. *They are going to be more than demanding.*

"In ten," she repeated and went to help prepare tea.

Felicity and Jennifer were in the kitchen putting away the items they had brought from the store. Hettie had not returned from drawing the bath for Miss Priscilla.

"Come," said Julia to the girls, "give me a hand with the tea things. Hettie has been waylaid running a bath for our guest."

"I thought you said they had grown children," said Felicity.

"They are. At least twenty, I think."

"Then why—?" began Felicity, but she was stopped short by one look at her mother.

"Because, it seems the dears are used to being waited on hand and foot," Julia replied. "I'm afraid we are in for some trying days."

The girls exchanged nervous glances, then busied themselves arranging the tea tray and preparing the plate of sweets.

"And I think it might be wise if you said 'ma'am' and 'sir' when addressing them," advised Julia. She had never before asked her children to act as servants—only as equals—caring for the needs of others.

Both girls showed their surprise.

"Well," Julia apologized, "we do need the money, and the longer they stay the more money we will make. You both need new dresses badly."

It was the first time Julia had mentioned to the girls their need of clothes.

"We'll try to remember," said Jennifer.

Hettie puffed into the kitchen, her face red.

"Dear little Miss Priscilla," she scoffed. "Miss Prissy, if you ask me!"

Julia had never seen her housekeeper so upset.

"First it's too cold—then it's too hot. Huh! Goldilocks herself had nothing on that one."

Julia tried to suppress a smile, and Felicity had a hard time stifling her giggle.

The sharp ring of a bell startled them all.

"What's that?" asked Julia.

"I'll go see," said Felicity, hurrying off to find the source of the noise.

It was not hard to do, for the bell rang persistently. Felicity found the answer in the parlor. Mrs. Blakeney, sitting in Julia's favorite chair, was shaking the daylights out of a copper bell.

"Is something wrong?" asked Felicity.

"We are ready for our tea," said the woman.

Fearing she would burst into laughter, Felicity did not dare answer. She turned and headed back to the kitchen. At the parlor door she remembered her mother's instructions and turned to say, as evenly as she could, "Yes, ma'am." Then she closed the door carefully, remembering to not let it slam, and hastened to the kitchen.

"You're not going to believe this," she said, her eyes big. "There Mrs. Blakeney sits, like a queen or something, ringing that noisy bell. There it goes again."

Julia picked up the tea tray and left the kitchen. Jennifer went to help her serve. The days ahead might indeed be trying.

"Miss Constance will let you know when Miss Priscilla is ready for her tea. She likes it weak—with both cream and sugar. And she prefers cake to cookies," said the woman as she accepted her cup of tea.

Julia nodded.

"We like to dine at seven," the woman went on. "And we will have breakfast served in our rooms when—"

"No," Julia interrupted, firmly but softly. "Breakfast is served in the dining room at seven-thirty or eight, whichever you prefer."

Though taken aback, the woman recovered quickly. "Eight will be fine," she said a bit sharply.

Julia turned to leave, and Jennifer followed. *Perhaps I should have humored her,* Julia thought. *We do need the money, and she is a paying guest. But no. It has gone quite far enough. We simply can't cater to them all day long.*

As soon as the door separating the parlor from the dining room closed behind them, Jennifer whispered, "Good for you, Mama."

Julia allowed herself a weak smile. She hoped she hadn't done the wrong thing.

When they reached the kitchen, Felicity was waiting for a report. Jennifer was happy to fill her in.

"She just sits there and gives orders," she concluded.

"Oh, to have Mrs. Williams back again," breathed Felicity, and the others laughed.

"She was strange but sweet," admitted Jennifer.

"I wonder where they are—and how they are," said Julia, setting the tea tray on the kitchen table and taking the cups to the sink. "Jennifer, get the smaller tray and set it up for Miss Priscilla. Felicity, get the flowered sugar and creamer from the sideboard. She might be calling any minute."

"I wonder what kind of a bell *she* has," Jennifer commented as she completed her task.

"Likely a gong," replied Felicity, and the two girls laughed together.

It was some time before Miss Constance rapped on the kitchen door to say that Miss Priscilla was ready for tea. Apparently she liked a long, leisurely soak.

"I'll send it right up," Julia promised.

"No need for you to run up with it. I'll take it."

Looking up in surprise, Julia looked into eyes full of deep sorrow. Her heart went out to Miss Constance. She wanted to step forward and pull the young woman into her arms. But the moment quickly passed, and Julia turned her attention to the task at hand. She added steaming water to the teapot, set it on the tray, and passed the tray to the young woman.

Miss Constance left the kitchen, her back straight, her chin up.

"My," remarked Julia, when the door had closed, "have you ever seen a sadder looking face?"

"Is she the maid?" asked Felicity.

"No," answered Julia. "The letter said the Blakeneys have two grown daughters."

"So, why do they pamper one and work the other?"

"I don't know," admitted Julia, shaking her head. "Of course, it may not be that they work her. Perhaps she just offered to carry the tray, this once, to save us the steps."

"Sure different from the rest of the family," observed Jennifer.

"She's awfully quiet," said Felicity.

"She was quiet in the parlor too," Jennifer added. "I never heard her say one thing over tea. Did you, Mama?"

"No, I guess I didn't," admitted Julia.

"The mother—now, she prattled the whole time," Jennifer explained to Felicity. "I don't know who she was talking to. No one was listening. But she talked without stopping."

"They are even more strange than poor Mrs. Williams," said Felicity. "That's what I'm thinking."

"Remember, girls," cautioned Julia. "Don't judge too soon—or too harshly. We really don't know anything about them yet."

Chapter Twenty

Getting Acquainted

As the week passed, Julia discovered that the twins had accurately summed up the Blakeney family on the day of their arrival. Mrs. Blakeney *did* talk all the time, and no one listened. In fact, Mr. Blakeney paid little attention to any of the women. He was stiff, bored, and not very courteous. Miss Priscilla whined or primped, and Miss Constance ran all errands not assigned to the "servants."

Julia wondered at the strange family arrangement but never mentioned her thoughts to her daughters. The girls openly discussed the situation, however, concocting stories to explain the circumstances.

"I'll bet she's a stepdaughter," said Felicity.

"But whose? His or hers?" asked Jennifer.

"She must be his daughter. He doesn't talk to anyone, but Mrs. Blakeney would talk to Constance if she were her daughter."

"She *does* talk to her—Constance just doesn't listen," Jennifer reminded Felicity.

"You're right. Mrs. Blakeney *does* talk."

"Maybe Constance was adopted."

"She looks too much like Priscilla."

"She does, doesn't she? Though I am sure Priscilla would die if you told her that."

Felicity mimicked the airs of Priscilla. "You're right.

Priscilla sees herself as much prettier."

"She is a little prettier," admitted Jennifer, "though I think Constance might be just as pretty—maybe even prettier because she isn't as pouty—if she weren't so stern."

"And wore her hair a little softer."

"And chose prettier dresses."

"That's enough," Julia cut in. "This is none of our business. Let's be kind," she reminded her offspring.

The girls washed the remaining dishes with fewer comments.

"It *is* strange," Hettie remarked after the girls slipped off to the porch swing with glasses of lemonade.

"It certainly is, but you know how some families are. For one reason or another they favor one child over the others."

Hettie too had seen it happen.

The back door opened, and the twins entered the kitchen, their glasses still full.

"Is it windy out?" asked Julia.

"No," grouched Felicity. "Miss Prissy has the swing." The girls often called the young woman by the name Hettie had used on the day she arrived.

"She wants some lemonade too. With cookies," Felicity continued.

Jennifer placed two glasses and some cookies on a tray and left with it.

Julia turned to Felicity. "Was her mother with her?"

"No."

"Constance?"

"Constance *was* there, but she had to run back to the room for Miss Prissy's shawl."

Julia was glad Jennifer had included lemonade for Miss Constance too. She felt sorry for her.

"Is Miss Prissy all settled?" Felicity asked when Jennifer returned.

Jennifer nodded. "She even said, 'Thank you kindly.' "

"Miss Prissy?"

"No. Not her. Miss Constance. 'Thank you kindly,' just like that. I've hardly heard her speak before."

"Mama," said Felicity, "how old do you think she is?"

"Well, I don't know," responded Julia, rolling another circle of pie crust dough. "Perhaps twenty-one or twenty-two."

"And Miss Prissy?"

"A couple years younger maybe."

"Miss Prissy looks bored to death," observed Jennifer.

"I suppose Miss Constance would be bored too if she didn't have all those books to read," Felicity stated. "But she is bound to run out soon. I wonder what she will do then?"

"We have a fine library. She is welcome to read any of our books," said Julia.

"She sure is different from her sister," Jennifer said as she stirred the lemon slice in her drink. "She doesn't say much, but she always makes her own bed, hangs up her clothes, and opens her window to air the room. Miss Prissy would never do that."

"But Miss Prissy talks more," said Felicity.

"If you call giving orders talking," Jennifer stated.

"Or whining," added Felicity.

"Now, girls. We have talked about this before," scolded Julia. "I don't want you saying nasty things about people."

"Even if they are true?" asked Felicity.

"Even if they are true," replied Julia.

————

The next day Jennifer and Felicity left the kitchen carrying pails. They found Miss Constance alone on the porch swing reading. She looked up when she heard them approach. Her eyes rested on the buckets.

"Do you milk cows?" she asked.

"Oh no," laughed Felicity. "We buy our milk from the Shannons."

"Do you carry it home like that?" she continued her probing.

"No, Tom gets it," answered Jennifer. "We are going to pick berries."

"Berries? Here?"

"No. Not in our garden. Wild berries."

"Where?" asked Miss Constance.

"It's a ways from here. In the woods. We know almost every patch around, I guess. Mama sends us out for berries, and she makes jams and jellies."

"Would you like to come?" asked Felicity.

Jennifer gave her a nervous look. Millicent was going along, and Jennifer had hoped to talk with her about the questions she had been asking.

"Oh, could I?" Miss Constance asked. "I have never picked berries before."

Felicity and Jennifer exchanged glances. "I'll get another pail," said Jennifer.

"I'll get it," said Felicity. "You go with Millicent. We'll meet you at the patch."

Jennifer gave her twin a grateful look.

"Do you have some walking shoes?" Felicity asked Miss Constance.

"I'll get them. And leave a note for Mother."

Felicity returned to the kitchen for another bucket. "I can't believe it," she told her mother. "Miss Constance wants to go with us. She has never picked berries before."

"Perhaps she will enjoy the outing," said Julia, who always found a quiet stroll through the trees relaxing.

Felicity took the pail and waited on the porch for Constance. She didn't have to wait long. The young woman hurried toward her a few minutes later, her cheeks pink with anticipation. Felicity had never seen her show any excitement before.

Felicity led the way down the winding path through the tall timber. "It's a bit of a walk," she explained. "I hope you don't mind."

"Oh no," said Constance. "I love walking."

The comment surprised Felicity. She had not seen the young woman walk anywhere.

"Walking is about the only way to get around here," Felicity explained. "We don't have roads for teams or motor cars."

"It's nice and quiet," responded Miss Constance.

"Is that why you came?" asked Felicity.

The girl hesitated. At last she replied, "We came for Priscilla. She needs a quiet place."

"Has she been ill?"

"You might say that," Miss Constance answered after another pause.

Felicity looked at her walking companion. *Surely Priscilla is not another escapee,* she thought. *She seems so—so normal—in a grumpy kind of way.* Putting her thoughts aside, Felicity responded, "I'm—I'm sorry to hear that."

Miss Constance was looking off in the distance, breathing deeply of the smell of pine and spruce. "Are there any bears here?" she asked.

Felicity hesitated. She didn't want to lie, but she didn't want to scare her companion either. After a short battle in her mind, honesty won. "Yes," she answered. "That's why we talk or sing when we walk—or rattle our pails or something. If they hear us coming they don't stay around."

Miss Constance laughed. It was the first time Felicity had heard her express any feeling of happiness. It sounded a little tight and strained, as though she was out of practice, but it was definitely a laugh.

"I think I'll like it here," she said.

"Are you staying longer than two weeks?"

A strange look crossed the girl's face; then she nodded slowly. "I expect so. Unless Priscilla just can't bear it."

Felicity wondered at the remark, but didn't question Miss Constance.

They beat Jennifer and Millicent to the patch and were busily filling their pails with plump, juicy berries when the other two girls arrived.

"How are they?" called Jennifer.

"Delicious!" answered Miss Constance. Stains on her lips proved that she spoke from firsthand knowledge.

Jennifer and Millicent found their own spot for picking and fell to work without conversation. Occasionally a bird flew over and loudly scolded the pickers for usurping the patch. They paid little heed to the chattering. Squirrels added their complaints from nearby trees. Chipmunks dashed into the patch and helped themselves, as if afraid there would be no berries left for them if they didn't hurry.

Hearing Miss Constance sigh, Felicity turned to look at her. She was sitting quietly, her hands motionless in her lap, her face upturned, studying the scudding clouds.

"It's getting hot," observed Jennifer. "I'm thirsty."

"Me, too," said Millicent. "Let's get a drink."

"Did you bring water?" asked Miss Constance, returning from her reverie.

"No—we just go to the stream over there."

"There's a stream?"

"You can hear it if you listen carefully," said Jennifer, tipping her head.

"Oh yes. I hear it. I didn't realize what that sound was. Can we go?"

"Sure. But take your berries with you. Some animal might get into them if you leave your bucket behind."

Miss Constance laughed again, a little freer now, as if she were beginning to find pleasure in life.

That afternoon at tea Mrs. Blakeney announced they would be leaving. Julia was disappointed. She had hoped for a bit more income from the family—even though they did keep her running with their multitude of orders.

"Send one of the young girls to help me pack in the morning," Mrs. Blakeney ordered.

Julia promised she would.

"Do you need them both?" she asked, trying to be helpful.

"Oh, I think one should be able to handle it just fine—unless she is dreadfully slow," said Mrs. Blakeney. "I just have the two suitcases."

"And your daughters?" asked Julia, unable to believe that Miss Prissy, who hadn't lifted a pretty pink finger since her arrival, would actually pack her own luggage. Unless, of course, poor Miss Constance would be packing for her.

"The girls! Oh, they aren't leaving," answered Mrs.

Blakeney as though Julia should have known.

Julia stared at the woman, who kept talking without even a pause.

"It will work just fine. I know Priscilla is bored, but she must endure that. She knew it would be this way. Constance will see to her."

Julia still had not thought of anything to say.

"Mr. Blakeney and I will be getting back to the city. There are so many events to attend to. I just can't be away very long at a time. You understand. Things are always so busy in the city. Especially when one is a social leader, so to speak. I will try to find time to pop out now and then to see how the girls are doing."

Chapter Twenty-one

Decisions

"Mama! Mama!" Jennifer cried as she rushed into the kitchen. "Millicent decided. Millicent decided!"

Julia stopped slicing bread. "That's wonderful!" she exclaimed, knowing exactly what her daughter meant. She took Jennifer into her arms.

"She said she thought about it and thought about it—and then she decided to ask God to forgive her sins—and to make her ready for heaven."

Felicity joined in the celebration. "That's great, Jen," she bubbled, getting in on the hugs.

"We should pray for her and help her in every way we can," said Julia.

"She promised to come to all the Bible studies."

"Does she have a Bible of her own?" asked Julia.

Jennifer shook her head.

"Then we must find one for her," said Julia. "I'm sure we have an extra one we could give her."

"Where is Papa?" asked Jennifer. "I want to tell him the news too."

"He and Tom are helping Mr. and Mrs. Adams get ready for their move. You may run and tell him. But Jennifer, do it discreetly. Millicent should be allowed to share her own good news with others. Do you understand?"

Jennifer nodded and was off to find her father.

"My! What excitement," said Julia. "But we do have guests to attend to. Felicity, would you get the cream for the tea tray? And fill the sugar bowl again, please."

"When are they leaving, Mama?" asked Felicity as she went to get the cream.

"On tomorrow's train. But the young ladies are staying on—for I don't know how long."

"I'm beginning to like Miss Constance," stated Felicity. "If she were given half a chance, I think she could be downright pleasant."

"Well, then," Julia said, "let's give her a *whole* chance. What do you say?"

Felicity grinned in reply.

They served the tea to Mr. and Mrs. Blakeney. As usual, Miss Priscilla stayed in her room. Miss Constance chose to take a bath after her outing to the berry patch rather than have tea in the parlor.

Mrs. Blakeney spoke to Julia over her cup of tea. "I have been admiring those silver candlesticks in the dining room. I have never seen any quite like them. I told Mr. Blakeney that you surely didn't get them here."

"No," smiled Julia, amused at the woman's forthrightness. "They came from the East. They were a wedding gift."

"So, you are from the East?"

"I was raised in Montreal. My papa still lives there."

Mrs. Blakeney nodded her head toward Mr. Blakeney as though to say, "I told you so."

"I like the candlesticks very much," continued Mrs. Blakeney. "How much are they?"

Julia fumbled for a response. Her first impulse was to tell her guest the candlesticks were not for sale. But Julia remembered the painting from the front hall. She would never have sold it had she been properly asked. Yet it was gone and life continued, and the money had helped them through a difficult time. She was sure life could go on without the silver candlesticks as well. She turned to her guest.

"They are really—quite expensive," she answered.

"I judged that," responded Mrs. Blakeney, as though Julia had insulted her.

"I hadn't considered selling them, but if I were to consider it—I would ask—" Julia thought quickly. *If Mrs. Blakeney really wants my candlesticks, she will not have them for one penny less than they are worth.* Having thought it through, Julia named a rather outrageous sum.

Mrs. Blakeney did not flinch. She turned to her husband. "You see," she said smugly, "I told you they could be had. Pay her." Then she looked at Julia. "I shall want to take them with me tomorrow," she said. "See that they are wrapped carefully."

Julia assigned the task to Hettie. She didn't have the heart to bundle the candlesticks herself. Later, as she fingered the money paid for the purchase, Julia had the sense to thank God for meeting their needs. Then she blinked away the sentimental tears.

———

"You asked her for how much?" John choked as he and Julia talked in the darkness after retiring.

"She didn't even blink," replied Julia, with some resentment.

"She gave it to you?"

"Well, not exactly. She ordered her husband to give it to me, and he did."

"You have the money?"

"I put it in the strong box in your desk drawer," said Julia.

"Well, the money will certainly help, but I'm sorry you had to let the candlesticks go," John sympathized. "I know they were important to you."

Julia allowed the silence to snuggle in around them and then she said, "Not as important as my family." She paused a moment before proceeding. "And that brings me to another subject I've been thinking about, John. It has to do with the girls. They need more schooling, and I don't think I—we— are able to teach them much more. They need a real school."

"I've been thinking too," John cut in. "And I've been

meaning to talk to you, but it's been difficult to find a minute alone when we aren't both exhausted."

Julia tilted her head so she could see his face, but in the darkness she could barely discern the outline.

John continued. "I wrote a letter a while back. To Mr. Small. He has been in touch two or three times since the mill moved, you know, asking me if I wanted a job. Well, that was some time ago—but I thought it wouldn't hurt to ask if he still has anything open."

Silence again.

"Others have done it. Gone out for seasonal work, I mean. I could come and go on the train while you and the girls stay here. Maybe we could afford a tutor if I had a paying job. It wouldn't be for long—"

That's what has been troubling John, thought Julia. *He knows we are short of funds even with my few guests. Yet he is hesitant to seek work because it will mean splitting up the family.* Julia's heart constricted. She didn't want to split up the family either. The thought of it frightened her. Yet she had been about to propose the same thing. Julia forced her thoughts back to what John had been saying.

"Have you heard from him?" she asked as evenly as she could manage.

"Not yet, but I just sent the letter a few days ago."

Julia reached for John's arm in the darkness. She needed an anchor.

"I was thinking," she said slowly, "that maybe we should send the girls away for a year of school."

"But that would cost a fortune," John began. "Even with me working and money from the guests—how could we afford—?"

"By sending them to Papa," Julia interrupted.

"To your father? Way back East?"

"He would love to have them, and it wouldn't cost us much. Papa would insist on having them as family, and they could attend the same finishing school I did. It's nearby and it's a good school."

"Have you talked to the girls about this?"

"Oh no. No. I'd never do that without talking to you first," said Julia, a bit offended.

John relaxed somewhat, but Julia could still feel the tension in his body.

"It means a lot to you, doesn't it?" he asked at last.

Julia thought a moment. "Well, yes and no," she said finally. "If you mean 'it is important to me that the girls go to the same school I attended,' then no. No, that doesn't matter. In fact, I had never even considered it before there was a need to find schooling—somewhere. But if you mean 'it is important to me to have them educated,' then yes, it is. And Papa is the only answer I can come up with."

John lay in the darkness thinking. "Do we have to decide right now?" he asked softly.

"No. Not tonight. But it is time for the first term to start. They will already be late—even if we send them now. We shouldn't delay if—"

"Let's try to have an answer about this by the weekend."

"Besides," said Julia slowly, "Papa always coaxes in his letters for some of us to come."

"But what about their clothes?" John asked. "They are hardly fit to attend a fashionable school in the East."

"I've thought of that," Julia admitted. "We could send the money from the candlesticks with them, and Papa could see that they are properly dressed."

"They need so many things. Would that be enough?"

"If it isn't, Papa will see to the rest."

"Julia, you know I don't want your father to have to dress my family."

"Oh, John!" exclaimed Julia. "He has so few pleasures. Would you deny him that as well? After all, they are his family too."

John reached out in the darkness and drew his wife against his side. "Of course they are," he murmured into her hair. "Of course."

————

Mr. and Mrs. Blakeney left on the morning train. Ac-

cording to Hettie, Miss Priscilla carried on "something awful." Miss Constance took their leaving in stride, though she
didn't look happy about the situation.

"Whatever will I do without Mama?" wailed Miss Priscilla.

"I will be here," said Miss Constance.

"But you always have your nose in a book," accused Miss
Priscilla.

"Perhaps you would do well do stick your nose in one
occasionally," said Miss Constance without sympathy. And
Miss Priscilla cried more loudly.

———

The community gathered for a potluck dinner on the Harrigan lawn to say farewell to the Adams family. Mrs. Adams
wept as she bid her friends goodbye.

"I will miss you all so much," she sniffed.

"You must write," said Julia. "We will want to know all
about your new home—Victor's job. The church you find. We
are going to miss you too."

The neighbors helped load the Adams' belongings onto
the outgoing train, and the family climbed aboard. Mrs. Adams clutched her small valise and the hand of one child. Mr.
Adams carried the bulging suitcase and gripped the hand of
the second child. And then the train was hissing and strain-
ing, ready to be off. Mr. and Mrs. Adams waved through the
window to those who had been part of their lives for so many
years.

———

With Mr. and Mrs. Blakeney gone, the Harrigan household soon settled into a new routine.

Miss Priscilla kept more and more to her room, and Miss
Constance continued to insist upon waiting on her. As Miss
Priscilla became more recluse, Miss Constance became more
friendly. She even came to the kitchen when it wasn't time
to pick up a tray for her sister. At Julia's invitation, she also
joined them for tea. On one of those occasions she had begged

them all, "Please don't call me Miss. Just call me Constance."

"I like her," Julia remarked later to Hettie and the girls. "We must be especially kind to her. I have a feeling she has not had an easy life. Though she has never indicated . . ." Julia let her remaining thoughts go unspoken and turned her attention to the other sister.

"We must watch out for Miss Priscilla too. It would be unthinkable for us to let her lie in her room and fade away if she is ill. I wish we saw more of her so we might judge her condition a bit more accurately." Julia decided to find some reason to call on Miss Priscilla often enough to keep an eye on the situation.

When Julia made her first visit she found Miss Priscilla sitting up in bed, nibbling cookies, and filing her nails.

"Is there anything I can do for you?" asked Julia politely.

The young woman sighed, "Just make the weeks go faster."

"I'm afraid I can do little about time," Julia smiled. "Though I have found that keeping oneself occupied makes time *seem* to pass more quickly."

Miss Priscilla scowled. "And how is one to be 'occupied' in this forsaken town?"

"Well, there are some nice paths to walk. There are little shops along Main Street. We still have one mercantile in town. And handwork can be interesting."

Miss Priscilla rolled her eyes.

Later in the day, however, Julia saw the young woman go for a walk down a forest path.

Chapter Twenty-two

Discoveries

"But we don't even know Grandfather!" Felicity wailed.

"I know," said Julia, tears in her eyes. "But he is a very gentle man. You will learn to love him just as I do."

"Couldn't you come with us, Mama?" pleaded Jennifer. "It's been ages since you have seen him."

"No," replied Julia. "Perhaps someday, but not just now."

"Do you think they will take us at that school?"

"I am sure they will. You are both good students—and fine young ladies."

"But what about—our dresses?" asked Jennifer, looking down at her ill-fitting, unstylish gown.

"We have money for shopping," replied Julia.

"What do you think, Papa?" asked Jennifer, turning her eyes to John.

"I think your mama is right. You deserve a good education—your grandfather has been yearning to get acquainted with you. He lives all alone in that big house. This seems like a perfect opportunity."

"But what about Christmas?" whispered Jennifer.

"It—it will be difficult for us. But by then you will have made friends—and will be feeling at home with Papa. And we do have the mail. We can send our gifts," said Julia, trying hard not to let her true feelings show.

"Well—it is exciting," declared Felicity. "I mean, we have

never been East—never been out of our town much. Are you sure we'll know how to act?" She giggled at the thought of making some ridiculous social error.

"You are your mother's daughter," John assured her. "You would not be more of a lady had you been raised in a palace." John meant every word. He had no fear that his daughters would embarrass themselves with bad manners.

Felicity knew he was right. Their mother had taught them to behave properly. The idea was becoming less frightening and more appealing.

"Oh, Jen—let's!" she cried suddenly, and threw her arms around her twin.

Jennifer allowed a slow, crooked smile to curve her lips. "All right, let's," she finally agreed, and the girls rushed to embrace their mother and father.

————

A letter came for John from Mr. Small. He was pleased that John had at last agreed to seek employment with him again. "I have work for you as soon as you are available," he wrote. "Just let me know the date of your arrival and the accommodation needed. If you need an advance for moving expenses, I will forward it immediately."

Mr. Small apparently assumed the whole family would be moving.

The news relieved John's tension somewhat, but he knew the solution was only temporary. He still needed to figure out a way to reunite his family.

Julia kept her mind off the coming separation by keeping herself busy. There was much to do to get the girls ready, and she had only a few days in which to do it.

John purchased the train tickets and got the luggage ready. Julia surveyed her closet and chose four gowns she could alter to fit her daughters. It left her short—it had been some time since she had been shopping for herself—but she had no place to go anyway, and the gowns were much too fancy to wear in the kitchen.

Julia sewed for two days, taking only a few hours for

sleep. She remodeled, patched, made over, and made do. She had little to work with, but when she finished the girls had suitable garments to wear on the train. After that it would be up to Papa.

Julia had wired him, and his return message revealed that his excitement more than matched that of the girls.

In her previous letters, Julia had written nothing about their hardships. *It would only worry him,* she told herself. *And he would surely send money—and that would nearly kill John.*

Julia had told him the mill had moved. And he knew Julia was hoping to keep her lovely home by sharing it with guests, and was indeed striving to make their entire town attractive to tourists. But Julia provided no further details.

As Julia worked anxiously to prepare her daughters for a time with their grandfather, her tears often fell on the material. She hoped with all her heart that the three would fall in love. She hoped her father understood her great love for him as she sent to him her most precious possessions. She hoped too that her girls would see in him all of the goodness, kindness, and wisdom she had always found. Julia prayed and prayed as she stitched. Her papa, whom she loved dearly, had not yet made his peace with God.

The time is getting short, Julia often reminded herself as she had reminded him in the past. But whenever she wrote to him of her concern, his return letters responded to every part of her letter except the paragraphs about his spiritual condition.

Perhaps Jennifer . . . Julia thought. *She shared her faith with Millicent. Perhaps she will be able to explain her faith to her grandfather—in her own simple way.* The thought made Julia pray even more diligently.

————

The day of the girls' departure came all too quickly for Julia. Felicity had thrown all fear and concern to the wind about five minutes after hearing of the plan. Jennifer accepted the idea more slowly. But by departure time, she too felt only excitement.

"You will write often?" Julia said as both a question and a statement. The girls had lost track of how many times she had reminded them.

"We promise," they replied in chorus.

"And to me too?" John added. He would be leaving the next day for the lumber camp.

"We promise," the girls repeated.

"I will miss you so," Julia said, her voice catching in her throat.

"We will miss you both too," they assured, but their attention had already turned to the train. They were eager to get aboard. The girls took turns embracing their mother and father.

"One more kiss," said Julia, kissing the two soft cheeks, "and one for each of you to give Grandfather from me."

And then in a flurry the girls were gone. It all happened too quickly for Julia. One minute she was holding her two daughters; the next minute the train was chugging away, leaving her empty and alone. She watched the white handkerchiefs waving from the windows until they were out of sight.

Then she turned to John and let the tears flow freely. He held her tightly, wishing with all his heart that he didn't have to leave the next day.

Julia soon straightened and looked into his eyes.

"We have done the right thing?" She worded it as a statement, but she pronounced it as a question.

John patted her shoulder. "We *have* done the right thing," he declared, and Julia found comfort in his reply.

————

The next morning it was even more difficult for Julia to let John go, but she tried not to cling to him. She did not want him to sense her great reluctance.

"I will try to get home for a weekend just as soon as I can," he promised.

"I have Hettie and Tom," Julia assured him. "I won't be alone."

"And the two guests," John reminded her. "They will keep you busy."

He was right about that. If Miss Priscilla had her way she would certainly keep Julia busy. Although the guests meant more work, Julia was grateful to have additional people in her house. It would not seem quite as empty.

"I will write," John promised, "every day," and he kissed her tenderly.

Julia could not answer.

"And you will be in my prayers—constantly," he continued.

Julia blinked hard to keep tears from spilling. She nodded her head and hoped John understood the depth of meaning in her silent communication.

"And remember—if you need me you can send a wire."

Julia nodded again, still unable to speak.

The train whistled, and Julia knew she had to let him go.

"I love you," she managed to whisper as he kissed her one last time. Then he too was gone.

Julia walked home alone. She did not hurry. She wanted to be in control of her emotions by the time she reached her kitchen. Hettie would have a strong, hot cup of tea waiting. Although the tea wouldn't do much for her emptiness, Hettie's company would help some.

Chapter Twenty-three

Deceived

Julia burst into the kitchen, tray in hand, cheeks flushed and her eyes snapping. She stopped at the kitchen table and set down her tray, fearing she would drop it in her agitation. But even after setting it down, she still gripped its edges.

Hettie waited for Julia to say something, but she just stared at the wall, her lips tightly drawn.

"What is it?" Hettie finally asked.

Julia lowered herself into a chair as if her legs would not hold her a moment longer.

"Miss—Miss Prissy!" exclaimed Julia, using the unflattering name for the first time. "She's—she's with child," said Julia, her eyes flashing.

Hettie nodded.

"You knew?" cried Julia.

"I suspected," said Hettie as she continued to peel potatoes.

"Well—well, I never! Who would have thought of such— The very idea—using my house—my Christian home—as a—as a hideaway."

Julia put her head in her hands, her shoulders trembling. Hettie went on removing potato peels.

"Well, I won't have it!" Julia declared suddenly. "Not in my house. I will not hide a woman who—who lived immorally and came sneaking off to me to hide her sin."

Hettie said nothing.

"She—she—oh, I'm so thankful the girls aren't here to see this," Julia wailed.

Hettie still made no reply.

"Why did she pick us? Why did she come here? There must be other places. But no. She had to choose us." Julia waved a shaking hand to show her disdain.

Hettie shifted her position, easing her weight from one foot to the other. Without lifting her eyes from the task before her, and without raising her voice, she responded, "Maybe she didn't choose us."

Julia's head came up. "Well—I mean—I know her mother chose us. Her mother runs everything in the family. If she spent more time training her daughters and less time being a—a social leader this—this—disgrace might not have beset her family."

"I didn't mean her mother," said Hettie slowly.

Julia looked puzzled. "Well, it certainly wasn't the father," she said. "I doubt he's ever made a family decision in his entire life."

Silence hung about them for a minute. Julia's face showed more and more impatience. "What are you trying to say, Hettie?" she asked at last.

"The woman is a sinner—just like you said," Hettie answered softly.

Julia's face flushed again. She was about to begin another discourse denouncing evil when she noticed a flicker in Hettie's eyes. "So what are you trying to say," Julia again demanded.

"How did our Lord feel about sinners?" asked Hettie, dropping the peeled potato in the pot. She picked up another and rinsed it in a pan of water.

Julia's eyes grew big. Her head dropped. Her trembling hands fluttered to her breast. "Oh, Hettie," she repented, "I just never thought . . ."

There was silence again while Julia did some soul searching. At last she lifted her head, her eyes tear-filled, her voice low.

"Do you think God sent her here for us to—to help—to love?" she asked.

"Could be."

After another long silence Julia nodded. "Yes, Hettie. It could be. And I nearly failed. Miserably."

"You would have gotten to it—sooner or later," Hettie comforted.

"I was about to send her away," Julia admitted.

"You might have thought of sending her away, but I doubt you could have done it."

"Oh, Hettie. I'm ashamed. So ashamed of my—my quick response. I was so angry. I felt so—so used."

"And so you were," said Hettie.

"Well, if God sent her to us, then we must do our best not to let Him down. We must somehow—somehow convince her that God can forgive—even this."

"It won't be easy," said Hettie, rinsing the pot of potatoes.

"You don't think she will be able to understand that God can forgive such sin?"

"No. I think it won't be easy to make her see that anything she takes a fancy to do, God would dare oppose," said Hettie. "She's a selfish, headstrong young woman if I ever saw one."

Hettie's thought was new to Julia. She paused to reflect on it. The assignment ahead would not be an easy one.

Chapter Twenty-four

Loving

"Are you still lonely?" Felicity asked Jennifer as they prepared for bed. When Jennifer failed to answer, Felicity responded to her own question with sisterly insight. "Me too."

Then the room was quiet again.

"It *is* nice to—to make Grandfather so happy," Felicity said.

Jennifer nodded and went on brushing her long hair.

The girls had settled into the new household quickly, at least by outward appearances. It hadn't been much different from their own, though Grandfather's larger house was more impressive and formal than their home in the mountains.

School was exciting. The girls were relieved to learn they were not far behind in their studies—and were every bit as refined and mannerly as their city peers.

But in spite of their doting grandfather's warm welcome, the acceptance of the other girls, and the shopping trips and entertainment, the empty feeling remained. They missed their parents. They missed home.

Felicity picked up her brush and swept it casually through her hair. "You know what I've decided?" she asked Jennifer.

Jennifer shook her head, afraid to trust her voice.

"I've decided to get married."

Jennifer's hand stopped in mid-stroke. She gave her twin a quizzical look. "You're *not* serious."

"I *am* serious. The only way to solve Mama and Papa's money problems is for one of us to marry a wealthy man. Since I don't suppose you will—I will."

"That's foolish talk," said Jennifer, no longer concerned. The idea was too preposterous to even consider.

"It's not foolish," Felicity shot back with a toss of her head.

"And where will you find this wealthy man?" asked Jennifer. "We go to a girls' school. We go straight to church and home again. Grandfather entertains people his own age. Where do you expect to meet anyone?"

"I'll manage it. Just wait."

Jennifer was unconvinced. "By the time men are wealthy, they are also old—and already married."

Felicity considered the comment. "There are young ones—who inherit," she insisted.

"Well, you certainly don't know any."

"I will. You'll see."

Jennifer laid aside her brush and went to turn down her bed. "Well," she flung at her twin, "if you find a young man— wealthy, a Christian, willing to marry you, and Mama and Papa decide you are old enough to marry—*then* you will have my blessing."

Felicity flipped back her long hair. "What makes you think I need your blessing?" she snorted. "I am doing this to save Mama and Papa and you talk like—"

"Mama and Papa do not need 'saving.' "

"Well, they need—need something—or we wouldn't be here while they are there," said Felicity, nearly in tears.

Jennifer felt like crying too. Loneliness crowded out her courage, making her feel deserted and desperate. "Let's not fight," she pleaded. She knew she could not stop her tears if she tried to say more.

Felicity turned her back. She did not want Jennifer to see how difficult it was to hold her own tears in check.

"You don't think it's a good idea?" Felicity finally managed to ask.

"No. And I don't think Mama and Papa would either. You are much too young even to be thinking of marriage."

"Other girls marry at our age."

"Other girls have not given it proper consideration."

"Then what *can* we do?" asked Felicity.

"Pray," Jennifer replied. "Just pray. And while we are at it—we must pray for Grandfather. Even though he's been taking us to church, I don't think he is a—a real believer."

Felicity had the same fear. "He's sweet, though, isn't he?"

Jennifer wiped her eyes with the sleeve of her white nightgown.

"He's very sweet," she agreed, then added, "and he must miss Mama something awful."

———

John pushed his chair away from the table in the cook shack and turned to leave for his own sleeping quarters. He shared the stark, simple shack with five other men. It was not the kind of arrangement he enjoyed.

It was noisy, crowded, and often filled with smoke. Although he was determined to endure the inconvenience, to live with the simplicity, and to forego his need for privacy, he continually longed for Julia.

John slowly strolled the short distance from the eating area to the shack. He wanted time to think—to pray. It was nearly impossible to pray with the raucous laughter, coarse jokes, and smoke-filled air pressing in on him. He stepped off the beaten path and lowered himself onto a fallen log. The night sky was clear, and stars were beginning to appear. John was weary. It had been a long, hard day of heavy work in the woods. He was a cutter now, not an overseer. Mr. Small had told him that would soon change, but for now John was working alongside the other men on the cutting crew. Actually, he figured the hard labor was good for him. The physical exhaustion kept him from thinking too many painful thoughts and made it easy for him to sleep at night despite his many concerns. And of course he was glad to have a paycheck coming regularly.

John turned his face toward heaven as his chest tightened with loneliness. Jule. The girls. Even the familiarity of his small town. He missed it all very much.

"God," he whispered into the darkening night, "I'm glad I didn't need to leave you behind too."

He sat silently, unable to go on. Even his prayers were painful. He watched the moon rise over the nearby pines. A cloud covered it for a moment. Then it reappeared, bigger and brighter than before. In the forest a wolf howled and another responded. They were on the hunt. They needed to survive. John felt a kinship with the wolves. He too was fighting for survival. For himself—but mostly for Jule. For the girls. He had to survive—for them.

———

Julia placed a late summer rose in a small vase on the breakfast tray she had prepared for Miss Priscilla. Constance had gone for a walk down one of the numerous wooded paths. Julia had assured the girl that her sister would be fine. Julia was quite able and willing to care for Priscilla's needs. Constance had looked relieved—anxious for a few moments alone. Priscilla was getting increasingly restless and difficult.

"I think a short walk would be good for Miss Priscilla too," Julia suggested.

"So do I," responded Constance with a weary sigh, "but she absolutely refuses."

Julia said no more. She had tried everything she could think of to make Miss Priscilla feel more comfortable—more content—more loved. But Miss Prissy was not an easy person to love. Determined to show her love no matter how difficult the task, Julia prayed more fervently for the strength to do so.

Julia lifted the tray. She did not look forward to the trip to Miss Priscilla's room. Along with the tray she carried another letter from Mrs. Blakeney. The woman had not made a single visit to see her daughters. Constance had told Julia that each letter from their mother apologized, but explained that she was too busy to come.

"That's the way it has always been with Mama," Constance said with little emotion. "We have long since become accustomed to it."

But Miss Priscilla did not seem used to it. She chafed and fussed and made life miserable for everyone whenever another promise was broken.

Julia rapped softly on the door.

"Yes," called Miss Priscilla, and Julia opened the door and walked in.

"Good morning," she said cheerfully. "Did you—?"

"Just set it down!" snapped Miss Priscilla. "I am famished. Where is Constance? She should have been here with the tray hours ago."

Julia let the words pass. She knew Miss Priscilla had awakened only a few minutes earlier. She and Hettie had been checking the room regularly.

"You have another letter," Julia said.

"From Mama?" Miss Priscilla brightened for a moment, and then turned glum. "I suppose she will tell me all about her most recent parties. I hate it. I hate hearing about all I am missing."

"You must like parties," Julia said as she poured coffee.

"I don't suppose you understand either. Constance never did. She just sat at home and read her old books—or worked in the flower beds or went to Ladies' Aid or something. Just like—like an old spinster."

Miss Priscilla spat out the last word. Julia guessed that spinster must be the most disagreeable term the girl could think of.

There were many things Julia wished to say in response but she held her tongue. "She seems happy," was all she said.

Miss Priscilla ignored the comment. She ripped open the envelope bearing her mother's letter and started to read. Her face suddenly brightened. "She's coming!" she cried. "She has her ticket. She is due on Thursday. That's tomorrow."

It was the first time Julia had ever seen the girl excited—rejoicing—over anything.

"We must wash and set your hair," Julia urged. Miss Priscilla had recently been refusing proper grooming. "Go ahead and eat your breakfast. I will come back and do it for you," Julia promised.

While working on Priscilla's hair, Julia encouraged her to come to the downstairs drawing room to greet her mother and have tea when she arrived.

"She won't do it," Constance warned later. "That would spoil the effect. She wants Mother to feel guilty for leaving her here alone—in her condition—and all that."

———

Mrs. Blakeney arrived the next day as promised. Right up until train time, Julia expected to receive some last-minute excuse. She was sure some social engagement would keep the woman away.

But she arrived. Bag and baggage. Julia heard her coming long before Tom opened the door for her.

Constance had been right. Priscilla refused to greet her mother in the parlor. Mrs. Blakeney went straight to Miss Priscilla's room. When Julia took up the tea tray, Miss Priscilla was sprawled on her bed, her hair a tangled mess around her pale face, and her eyes drained of all excitement or eagerness. She moaned each time she shifted position and fretted and scolded until Julia wanted to shake her.

"My poor baby," soothed Mrs. Blakeney, smoothing the girl's hair. "Constance—I trusted you to take better care of your sister. Look at her. Her nails look like they haven't been attended to in weeks and—"

Julia set down the tray and quickly left the room. She grabbed a shawl on her way through the kitchen and headed to the garden. "I wish—I wish there were potatoes to dig—or carrots to pull—or something!" she hissed. "I need to work off some steam."

But the garden had all been cared for by Tom. Winter was approaching. Julia's thoughts turned from the spoiled

Miss Priscilla to her own dear daughters and the long winter without them.

————

Mrs. Blakeney stayed for only a few days. Julia wondered if she found her daughter too disagreeable to endure. Before she left she purchased a porcelain pitcher and bowl and a small gilt-edged mirror from Julia. Julia didn't allow herself the pleasure of tears as she tucked the generous payment into the safe-keeping box in John's desk drawer. They needed the money. They could live without treasures.

————

Another month passed and Julia had another guest. His name was Dr. Martin Waters, and he came from some spot unknown to any of them. Mrs. Blakeney had hired him to be on guard until Miss Priscilla's baby came, to deliver the infant, and then to leave discreetly. This information came out little by little, for he had been given strict orders to keep silent about his mission.

Dr. Waters was very aware of his own presence, and he made certain that others were too. He wore flashy clothes, twitched his carefully trimmed mustache, and cast furtive glances as though fearful someone were following him. His steel blue eyes flashed impatience with the least provocation, and Julia sensed that he was very short-tempered.

Julia felt uncomfortable around him, but there was little she could do. Although difficult to endure, he was a paying guest.

Miss Priscilla seemed to like the idea of having a little male company, and she began ordering Constance to brush her hair and manicure her nails again. Dr. Waters, a man of about forty, was not without a measure of masculine appeal, and his silence and manner made him mysterious and intriguing.

Miss Priscilla may as well have saved herself the trouble, however. The doctor seemed to be interested in nothing except his fee—which likely would be sizable.

Dr. Waters kept mostly to himself and ignored the majority of Miss Priscilla's moans and groans and cries of complaint. He did care for her solicitously, however, handing out little pink or white pills with abandon. Julia feared for the unborn child, but dared not be too open with her comments.

"I just hope this whole ordeal is over quickly," she confided to Hettie. "It seems that our efforts to show love and understanding have been in vain. Miss Priscilla has not softened one bit. In fact, I fear she is even more disagreeable than ever. I don't know how poor Constance stands it."

"I think she has had years of practice," responded Hettie. "It's a clear case of the older, rational, responsible sister needing to care for the younger, spoiled, irresponsible one."

Julia felt that Hettie had summed up the situation well.

Julia did not get her wish for quick release from their circumstance. Miss Priscilla, in spite of her great impatience, failed to deliver on time. The days dragged by and everyone in the house became tense and edgy. Miss Priscilla fussed and scolded, screaming at anyone who entered her room and at anyone who did not come when she called.

Julia found it more and more difficult to keep her promise. The young woman was nearly impossible to love.

Chapter Twenty-five

Delivery

A sharp rap on the bedroom door awakened Julia. Then she heard a voice. "Mrs. Harrigan. Mrs. Harrigan. It's time. It's time."

Julia could make no sense of the words—or their urgency. She sat up in bed trying to get her bearings, trying to figure out who was calling and why.

"Mrs. Harrigan," the voice came again, sounding desperate. "Please come. Please hurry. It's time."

"It's Constance," Julia said. Then reality flooded over her. *The baby. It must be Priscilla and the baby.*

Julia arose swiftly and snatched a robe from the wardrobe. The generator had been turned off so they had no electricity. Julia didn't take time to light a lamp. She hastened to the door, tying the robe as she went.

Constance was about to rap again when Julia jerked the door open. "It's time," Constance said again, her hand still in midair.

"Does the doctor need anything?" asked Julia.

"Oh my!" exclaimed Constance, "I didn't think to call him." She turned and hurried down the hall toward the doctor's room.

His bedroom door opened before Constance reached it, and the man came out. He looked disgruntled to have his sleep disturbed—but Julia was thankful to see that he was prepared to take charge. His sleeves were rolled up and he carried his official-looking black bag.

"Is the kettle hot?" he asked.

Of course the kettle is not hot. It is one o'clock in the morning, Julia thought. But she kept her snippy answer to herself and said instead, "I'll see to it right away."

Julia closed her ears to the sounds coming from Priscilla's room and hurried down the stairs, through the house, and to the kitchen.

———

It was after eight when Constance came running to the kitchen to inform Julia that the delivery had gone well and that a baby boy had arrived.

Julia felt the excitement a new baby always brought to her. She wanted to run upstairs immediately to see the child.

"The doctor wants to know where to put him," Constance continued, and Julia's thoughts came back to earth with a jolt.

This is not a wanted baby, Julia reminded herself. *No one has prepared for his coming. Even I did not think to make any arrangements.*

"Why—why—" she stammered, "won't he be staying in Miss Priscilla's room?"

"Priscilla doesn't even want to see him," replied Constance, her voice breaking. "She wants him out of her room at once. She has turned her face to the wall."

"But—but surely—" But then she put everything together. Miss Priscilla had hidden for four months. She had never intended to return home with a child.

"I'll—I'll fix something. Bring him to my room."

"But—but I thought perhaps I could keep him in my room," Constance explained as they hurried through the house. "I—I don't know a thing about babies, but if you would be kind enough to—And if we had a bed—"

"I don't have a baby bed," Julia said, an edge to her voice. *Why hasn't Mrs. Blakeney made provisions?* Julia wondered.

She has been quite thorough in everything else. After all, the baby is her flesh and blood.

"Can we use a—a box—or a drawer—or something?" Constance asked, and Julia scolded herself for her angry thoughts.

Poor Constance, she thought instead. *This has all been so difficult for her, and now she must be a nursemaid to a baby as well.*

"We'll find something," she assured the girl.

Baby boy Blakeney was eventually dressed in a white gown with pink ribbons, bundled in used pink blankets, and laid in an emptied, towel-padded dresser drawer. Julia could have wept as she looked down on him.

"You poor little soul," she whispered. "You didn't ask to come into the world. And you certainly didn't get much of a welcome. What will happen to you? Whatever will happen to you? If only I could have had you to love—" Julia brushed away tears and went back to the kitchen to prepare hot tea for Miss Priscilla.

They had nothing for the new baby. Tom fashioned a nipple of sorts from the finger of a new glove. It was all Mr. Perry had in his store that would make any kind of feeding arrangement. Julia fixed a bottle of milk and fed the hungry baby.

Constance took over the care of the infant as Julia instructed her. There were no diapers, so Julia told Hettie to tear up an old flannel sheet. There wasn't even time to put in a proper hem.

Julia had never before felt so disturbed over the birth of a baby. Her heart cried, *It's not right. It's not fair. He wasn't at fault.* It seemed so totally wrong that a child should be born unwanted—unwelcomed—unloved.

But when Julia looked at Constance's face as she held the baby and coaxed him to drink from the makeshift bottle, she was forced to change her opinion.

I've been wrong, Julia concluded. *He may have been unwanted—but he is not unloved. Constance has already fallen in love with him.*

And it was true. Never did a baby get more tender care than Constance gave her new nephew.

"What do you call him?" Julia asked Constance one evening.

"Mother said he is not to be named," responded Constance with a sigh.

Julia could not disguise her surprise.

"But—secretly—I call him Peter," the young woman confided.

"Peter. I like it." Julia waited for Constance to finish feeding Peter and give him to her to hold.

———

"He seems to be doing well, doesn't he?" Julia said on one of her daily visits to see the baby. She lowered the small garment she was stitching for Peter and watched him sucking hungrily.

"He's a little piggy," laughed Constance in a way Julia had never heard her laugh before.

Constance kissed the top of the downy head. "I think he has grown already," she said. "Eight days old—and already bigger."

Julia smiled. "I can see it too. The way he eats, I guess he should." Then Julia added with a chuckle, "We are going to have to buy more gloves. I do hope Mr. Perry has another pair or two. We have already cut all the fingertips off the pair we bought."

Constance looked up. "Oh, it shouldn't be much longer," she said. "The doctor says Priscilla will be ready to travel soon."

Julia lifted her eyebrows in surprise.

"Will the doctor be traveling with you?" she asked.

"Oh no. He plans to go straight back to—wherever. He says his contract does not include escorting us home."

"I see," said Julia, but she still had many questions.

———

"I will be leaving tomorrow," the doctor announced at dinner the next evening.

Even Priscilla had joined them at the table. She still looked pale, but Julia believed that it was as much from shutting herself in her room, away from fresh air and sunshine, as from her recent delivery.

"I shall need clean garments and blankets for the baby and enough feedings to last for a twelve-hour trip."

Three heads lifted and three pairs of eyes studied the man's face.

"What do you mean?" asked Constance.

The doctor looked blank at her question. "I need clothes and food for the infant," he repeated. "Enough for a twelve-hour trip. Why is that confusing?"

"But you won't be taking the baby."

"Indeed, I will. I have instructions from your mother—"

"My mother doesn't understand the situation," Constance interrupted. "She made those plans long before—"

"I have my orders—and I plan to fulfill them," the doctor said adamantly.

"But you *can't* take the baby."

"I *must* take the baby—according to contract," the man declared.

"But—"

"Oh, Constance. For goodness' sake don't fuss," broke in Priscilla, tossing her napkin on the table and standing up. "You know the plan—the arrangement. Mother has it all cared for."

"But Mother doesn't know Peter!" cried Constance, also rising.

"Peter? Peter?" screamed Priscilla. "Who called him Peter? You know Mother said he wasn't to be named. What right do you have—?"

"I *love* him!" Constance shouted back at her screaming sister. "I *love* him."

Priscilla looked at Constance. Surprise and anger flashed across her face. Then she began to cry. Hot tears washed down her cheeks and made trails in her face powder.

"That's—that's—just like you!" she shouted at Constance. "You can't even be trusted to—to care for a baby. You know that Mother said he—"

"I *will* care for him. I will!"

"You will not bring that—that baby home. Do you hear? You will not!" Priscilla shouted.

Julia trembled. She had never witnessed such a quarrel. She wanted to cover her ears and flee, but she was rooted to the spot.

"Of course I won't take him home!" Constance shouted back at her sister. "I wouldn't dream of taking him to where—to that place. I will keep him here—for a while. I have money. I can find us a place."

"You're a fool!" yelled Priscilla. "You're a—a pigheaded, selfish fool." With that final burst of anger she fled the room, sobbing loudly.

Constance dropped back to her chair and reached for a napkin to press to her cheek. Her shoulders trembled, but Julia knew she felt that she had won the battle.

At length she lifted her head and looked at Julia.

"Is it—can I stay—for just a while? Just until I am able to make arrangements for me and—and Peter?"

"Of—of course," whispered Julia.

A stirring at the table reminded Julia they were not alone. She had forgotten the doctor.

"I'm afraid it's out of the question. I already have all of the papers in order for the adoption."

"But you can't."

"I can—and I will," the man said. "I have a legal document. Signed and binding. You will not interfere." He pushed back his chair and stood up.

"I want the child ready by nine o'clock," he said with authority. Then he looked directly at Julia. "Mrs. Harrigan—I expect you to see to it."

He stalked from the room, and Constance buried her face in her hands and sobbed.

———

The next morning when Julia went to check on Constance and Peter, she found a note.

> Peter had his morning feeding, and all his things are packed and ready to go. Give him one last kiss for me. I have gone for a walk. C.L.B.

Julia opened the door softly, brushing away tears. Peter lay sleeping in his makeshift bed. Beside him was a suitcase that belonged to Constance. In it, neatly folded, were all of the garments Constance and Julia had made over the past several days. The borrowed clothing that had belonged to Julia's two baby girls lay in an orderly stack on the bed.

Julia lifted the small baby from his bed to prepare him for his journey.

"She loves you—so much," she whispered to the sleeping child, her tears falling onto his blanket. "I only hope—only pray that your new mother—whoever she might be—will love you half as much."

Julia lifted the small bundle and kissed the soft cheek. The baby squirmed but did not waken.

"One from me—and one from Aunt Constance," whispered Julia as she kissed him again. She paused a minute to gain a measure of control before she took the baby to the waiting doctor.

————

Julia was pacing the kitchen floor, her brow furrowed, her lips moving in silent prayer when the door opened and Constance stepped in. Julia took one look at the young woman's face and moved to embrace her. They clung to one another for several minutes, neither one speaking. Shared tears were their only communication.

"You must be starved," Julia whispered. "You have been gone all day. Sit down. Hettie saved you a plate."

Julia pushed the teakettle forward on the stove and checked the warming oven that held the waiting food.

"Draw your chair closer to the fire," Julia urged. "It's cold out. You must be chilled through and through."

Constance wiped her eyes, blew her nose, and then did as Julia suggested.

"I walked with them to the train," Julia said hesitantly. "He was—fine. He never even awakened when the whistle blew."

Constance turned her face.

"The—the twelve hours will soon be up," Julia went on. "Just think of it. Somewhere—right now—there is a very excited woman—and man—waiting for that little one. Can you just imagine how they feel?"

Julia saw the sagging shoulders tremble.

"There was a time when we thought of adopting a baby boy. But we were told there weren't many children available for adoption. And because we already had two healthy girls it might be a long wait."

The young woman made no effort to respond. Julia stepped closer and placed her hand on the trembling shoulder.

"Constance, I am not trying to make it harder for you. I just want you to think about the other couple. How they might have prayed—longed for a baby. Little Peter could—will—make them very happy. He is such a sweet little thing. He will be loved. We'll pray for that. We'll pray that he has wise and kind and loving parents."

Constance wept again, but soon she looked at Julia and whispered, "You are right. He is better off with—with both a mother and a father. I loved him—will always love him—but I couldn't have given him the home he deserved. Oh, Julia, I need to learn how to pray so that I might pray for him. I know you know how. I have watched you—with me—with Priscilla. No one could have been as kind or as patient without—without a deep faith in God. Please—please tell me what I must do to find God in that way."

Through tears that blurred her vision, Julia led Constance in reading Scripture portions that explained how to believe in the Son of God.

————

Priscilla and Constance left the next day. Constance seemed reluctant to leave, but Priscilla was impatient to be gone.

"I suppose that poky old train will be late," she fussed, but the train was right on time.

"I will write," Constance promised.

"I will be waiting," said Julia.

"Thank you. Thank you so much—for sharing your faith—for understanding—for your love," said Constance.

Julia hugged her again and blinked back another onset of tears. She turned from Constance to Priscilla. The train was coming toward them, chugging heavily as it pulled up the incline toward the station.

"Priscilla," said Julia. "I—I'll continue to pray for you." Julia tried to give the girl a parting embrace, but Priscilla accepted only a token hug and then stepped back quickly.

"Constance, grab that big bag," she ordered, "it's much too heavy for me."

Julia turned back to Constance who welcomed the warmth of her farewell embrace.

"Don't let her upset you," whispered Constance. "She was affected by your love much more than she lets on. She said as much to me. And now that I know God—I will be able to help her. I will keep working and praying and—who knows?"

Chapter Twenty-six

Family

Winter's snow arrived early, making Julia feel buried and confined in the big, empty house. If she had not had Christmas projects to keep her mind and fingers busy, she felt sure she would have gone out of her mind with loneliness and sorrow.

John came home for Christmas, and Julia clung to him as if he were her only link to sanity. "I have been counting the days ever since you left," she moaned, "but they ticked by so slowly."

John pulled her close and brushed his lips against her hair.

"You've lost weight," Julia fretted.

"Not much."

"But you *have* lost weight. Aren't the meals—?"

"The meals are fine. They feed us like—like lumberjacks," John said with a grin.

Julia lifted a hand to rub his cheek. "It's so good to have you home."

But strangely, having John home made her ache even more intensely for Jennifer and Felicity—or perhaps it was because of Christmas. Julia's thoughts kept returning to the girls.

It will be such a special Christmas for Papa, she kept telling herself. She pictured the big house on St. Pierre. The staff would have decorated the halls with boughs of cedar and holly. The tree would be standing in the wide front parlor, hung with ornaments too numerous to count. Cinnamon and nutmeg would fill the house with irresistible aromas. Julia remembered it all. It would be as it had been during her childhood. Having the girls this year gave her papa a reason to celebrate Christmas.

"Oh, if only we could be there too," grieved Julia. "Then— then I would be so happy."

But they were not there. Julia mailed her parcels with teary eyes and a loving heart. Then she busied herself baking John's favorite desserts, hanging the familiar streamers, and carefully placing the glass balls on the tree John brought home to her.

On Christmas day Julia set the table for seven. She had invited the Clancys and Mr. Perry for dinner. She had wanted to have everyone who was left in town, but the Shannon children had the measles and could not go out, and the Greenwalds had guests of their own.

John and Julia managed to get through the day. Julia tried to be cheerful, tried to keep her mind on her guests, but her thoughts kept slipping to her family in the East. *I wonder what they are doing now. I wonder if the girls are thinking of us. I wonder—*

And then the guests went home and the day was over. Julia was glad she had worked so hard to get ready. As bone-tired as she was, at least she would be able to sleep.

———

Julia was hard pressed to keep busy as the winter days came and went. The household needed many things, but she had no materials with which to work. Julia chose to be frugal. She stretched John's paychecks as far as possible so they could lay aside sufficient funds to reunite the family.

In February Hettie took sick. Julia worried more than she admitted. There was no doctor and no longer even a druggist in town. What few medications remained were shelved in Mr. Perry's back room.

"I really have very little to offer you," Mr. Perry told Julia when she asked for his help.

"I just don't know what to do," Julia sighed. "I have heard of poultices for chest colds and steaming for head colds—but this is neither. I don't know what is wrong with her."

"Well, keep her warm and quiet—that's about all I know," said Mr. Perry. "And chicken broth. My ma used to swear by chicken broth."

"And where am I to get a chicken? I have tasted nothing but wild meat for two years now."

The man nodded his head but said nothing more.

Julia picked up a few tablets said to bring relief from aches and pains and then trudged home through the snow.

It was several days before Julia saw any improvement in Hettie's condition. By then Julia was exhausted from work and worry.

"I'll sit with her," said Tom, entering the room. "You get some sleep."

Julia did not argue. She went to her room and fell on her bed without even removing her clothes. "Dear God, may she be all right now," she whispered, and then she slept.

———

In March the Clancys moved away.

"There's no need for a town clerk when there's no longer a town," Mr. Clancy said simply.

"I've been thinkin'," Mrs. Greenwald said to Julia a few days later. "No need to keep those shops open when there is nothing much in them. Might as well sort out what is left and board up those windows before everyone is gone and there's no one to help us."

Only the Shannons, the Greenwalds, and Mr. Perry were left.

"What about the summer trade?" asked Julia.

"Perhaps Mr. Perry will lend a shelf or two in his store," Mrs. Greenwald continued, and Julia didn't argue.

The few remaining hand-crafted goods were moved to Perry's store, and the men of the community nailed the boards back on the shop windows.

———

At last Julia began to feel that spring might actually come again. She took every opportunity to be outdoors, even though it was too early to plant a garden, too wet to walk in the woods, and too desolate to stroll downtown. Julia mostly puttered at home or hurried to the post office to see if she had a letter from John, the girls, or her father.

John's letters always sounded cheerful. True to his word, Mr. Small had found John a position as overseer so he no longer had to put in hard, heavy days as a cutter. He told Julia how the town was growing, with more and more homes lining the crooked streets.

"They have even put in electricity," he wrote in one letter. "Of course that is thanks to the lumber mill." He spoke often of missing his family and how happy he would be when he had saved enough money so he could come home again.

The girls' letters always told interesting incidents of life in the big city. They had learned to love their grandfather. They enjoyed school and the young ladies who had quickly become their friends. They wrote about their interests in music and sports, and they told Julia about shopping trips and visits to exciting places. But they also spoke of their eagerness to be back with their parents again. Julia could often detect little cries of loneliness.

Her father's hasty notes were filled with comments about the girls. He praised Julia for raising such fine young ladies, talked of their accomplishments in school, gloated over how well Jennifer was doing on the piano and how sharp Felicity was in mathematics. It was always a joy for Julia to read her father's letters—but they did make her even more lonely.

———

After Tom plowed the garden, Julia set out with her packets of seeds, glad to have something to do, something that would actually show growth—advancement. At the same time she wondered, *Why am I doing this? I am planting a*

garden big enough to feed the town—and there is only Hettie,
Tom, and me.

What about your summer guests? she argued with herself.

Guests? Perhaps a few—but never enough. Never enough
to earn a suitable income, and never enough to eat all of these
vegetables.

But Julia planted on. She felt compelled to do so. It kept
her feeling busy—profitable.

————

"We are leaving, too," Maude Shannon told Julia toward
the end of spring. "Jim just doesn't want to struggle here
anymore."

Julia didn't even raise her head. She had expected it.

"Do you want the cow?" asked Maude.

"I'll ask Tom. He would have to care for her. I will let him
decide."

"I'm sorry to leave you like this," Maude went on.

Julia managed a half smile. "That's all right," she said.
"We have always said that whenever a family feels they
should move—that it's time to go—then they should do so."

"Might you go too?" Maude asked.

Julia shifted. She had thought of it. Had wondered. Had
even hoped John might suggest it.

"No," she finally said. "No, I don't think so. Not now at
any rate."

"Do you have folks coming?" Mrs. Shannon asked.

"You mean summer guests? No, not yet—but it's still
early. Most folks don't come until late summer or early fall."

"Well, I should get going. I've got a lot to do," Maude said.
"Packin' and all. Thanks for the tea, Julia."

Maude started to leave but then turned back to Julia. "I
was wonderin'—before I go, could you—could you sorta say
a prayer for me. I'm—I guess I'm scared and—and worried
and I need some faith if I'm gonna get through this. I need
God, Julia."

With a sense of humility, Julia took her neighbor's hand.

"Of course, Maude. Of course. He's here. You only need to reach out to Him."

After praying with Maude, Julia followed her to the kitchen door and watched her go. Julia then turned to her garden. A few weeds were showing again.

————

John arrived home unannounced. He surprised Julia by walking up behind her and pulling her apron string as she hoed her garden. Startled, Julia whirled to see who would tease her in such a way. She could not believe her eyes. Throwing herself into his arms she wept on his shoulder.

"Why, I didn't even know—hadn't even received your letter—" she said when she could speak again.

"There wasn't any letter," John admitted. "I just—well I just had to see you, so I begged for a few days off."

"The Shannons have gone," Julia told him.

"I noticed. I saw the empty yard—the boarded-up windows."

"It's an empty town," said Julia, shaking her head. She turned her face to keep John from seeing the tears building up.

John led Julia to the porch swing and motioned for her to be seated. He eased himself down beside her. "Jule," he began slowly, "I've been doing a lot of thinking." He paused to choose his words carefully. He did not want to hurt the woman he loved so dearly.

"You have—have given it everything you could, but, Jule—I don't think it's going to work. Not here. I'm afraid we are going to have to give up, Jule. To let the house go."

John waited, holding his breath. He had never given Julia orders before. He expected a cry of protest, but Julia remained silent.

"We can't go on like this, Jule. I can't stand being without you—without the girls. I think—"

"What are you saying?" asked Julia, her voice trembling.

"We need to be together. To be a family again. I know it will hurt you to lose the house, but—"

"The house?" gasped Julia. "You think I can't give up the *house?*"

John looked at his wife, a puzzled expression in his eyes.

"John, I don't care about the house. Oh, I—I've loved it, of course—but without my family—the big, beautiful house has become a—a mammoth tomb. Empty and lonely. No, John, it isn't my love for the house that has kept me here—trying to—"

"Then what?" asked John.

"You. You, John. I thought you couldn't bear to give up the house. I didn't want to lose it—for you, John."

"You mean—?"

Julia nodded her head vigorously. "You worked so hard to give me everything—to have things perfect for me. I thought—I thought it would—would crush you to—to give it all up. I tried to hold it for *you*," sobbed Julia, burying her face against her husband's shoulder.

"Oh, Jule, Jule," John soothed her. "I just want—I just want you. I want us to be together. I can't stand this—this being apart."

"That's all I want too," sobbed Julia.

John kissed her wet cheek. He held her close, his own tears joining hers. Then he smiled and lifted her chin. "You'll come with me? Move? Now?" he asked.

"Oh yes!" cried Julia, her eyes beginning to shine.

"What of Hettie—and Tom?"

"Hettie's father just wrote. He wants them to live with him. He's not been well. Hettie was fussing about it because she wouldn't leave me."

John's arm tightened around Julia. "I found a little house," he enthused like a child. "It's—it's not much—nothing like this one—but it does have a mountain view."

Julia sensed his teasing. "Is there room for all of us?" she asked.

John nodded. "It will be crowded. The girls will have to share a room."

"They've always shared a room," Julia reminded him.

"Oh, John—I'm so—so filled with—with joy—I fear I might

burst. I can hardly wait another minute."

John kissed her again, his face sobering. "I was so afraid," he admitted. "So afraid you might not want to go off to another lumber town. That you wouldn't be able to leave— this." He nodded toward the large white house.

Julia shook her head with confidence. She was surprised that her long-troubled mind felt peace at last.

"It's time," she whispered. "I feel—feel free to go now. I didn't feel this way before. This—release. Why?"

"Perhaps because you were still needed here," John answered.

Julia thought of Constance and of Maude Shannon. "Yes, perhaps that *is* the reason," she said. "Maybe I *was* still needed here."

"And now?" asked John.

Julia placed her arms around his neck, her face aglow. "Now," she said, "now God is giving us new challenges. New adventures. Oh, John! I'm so thankful we can face them together."

"Let's go wire the girls," John suggested, and Julia hastily agreed.

"Perhaps Papa will bring them home to us!" she exclaimed, thinking ahead to the great reunion of their family. Tears of happiness glistened on her cheeks as she laid her head against John's shoulder.